Protected Mate

Catamount Lion Shifters, Book 1

By J. H. Croix

ISBN: 1530006341
ISBN 13: 9781530006342

Dedication

To the man of my dreams…who steals my heart every day.

Sign up for my newsletter for information on new releases!

http://jhcroix.com/page4/

Follow me!

jhcroix@jhcroix.com
https://twitter.com/JHCroix
https://www.facebook.com/jhcroix

Centuries ago in the northern Appalachian Mountains, mountain lions fled deeper and deeper into the mountains, seeking safety from the rapid encroachment of humanity into their vast territory. Mountain lions developed the power to shift from human to mountain lion and back again, saving their species as they hid in plain sight. The majestic wild cats became creatures of myth. Reported sightings were treated as wildly speculative rumors. Impossible. Until one evening on a busy highway, a car struck an animal in the dark. The first confirmed sighting of a mountain lion in the East in close to seventy-five years. The wild cat was dead, its unbelievable existence snuffed out by a car. This mountain lion wasn't just any mountain lion. Though its autopsy would only reveal it was, in fact, a mountain lion and that the lion had improbably traveled over 1,500 miles from South Dakota, the longest known journey for such a creature. In Catamount, Maine, shifters lived amongst the world, having successfully protected their very existence for centuries. Until one of their own died an improbable death, and they learned of a threat facing their kind.

Chapter 1

Dane Ashworth pushed through the swinging door of Roxanne's Country Store and found himself in a small crowd. Roxanne's was practically the center of the universe as far as Catamount, Maine was concerned. This morning, Roxanne, the owner, had the news on rather than her usual fare of talk shows. Dane looked up at the screen and saw the body of a dead mountain lion lying on the side of a highway—a majestic animal killed by a careless driver. His heart stuttered, and fear washed through him, confusion swirling in his thoughts. The reporter announced this was the first confirmed sighting of a mountain lion in New England since nineteen thirty-eight when a mountain lion was trapped in Maine. Eastern mountain lions had been declared extinct.

In Catamount, the hidden truth walked among everyone else—mountain lions had evolved to shift into human form centuries ago. The news switched to the autopsy scene with a veterinarian medical examiner. The examiner reported the cat in question had been tagged with a tracking device. Scientists were puzzled and stunned by

1

its results. The cat had traversed from the mid-west to the east in North America, traveling roughly fifteen hundred miles to Connecticut—twice as far as any previous known distance for a mountain lion.

It was only then Dane recognized the mountain lion was Callen, his sister's mate. Callen bore a distinctive scar on his neck. It was visible when the camera scanned over his body, lifeless on the stainless steel table. Dane closed his eyes, grief flashing through him. His sister would be devastated. Callen came from a long line of shifters and was considered one of the dominant male shifters in this area. In his human form, he traveled frequently and had recently traveled to South Dakota and Montana on multiple excursions to try to confirm if the rumors of shifters in that area were true.

How and why he was traveling in his mountain lion form through Connecticut was as much of a mystery as his death by car on a highway. Dane glanced around, finally catching the eye of Jake, a good friend. With a nod of his head, Dane walked back outside and Jake followed.

"What the hell is going on?" Dane asked flatly.

"I just walked in myself. Have you seen Shana? You'd better find her before she walks in here and sees his body on television like that," Jake replied.

Dane nodded sharply. "I'll go find her in a minute. What is everyone saying?"

"Everyone's freaking out. Why was he on foot, why was he in cat form, how come he didn't shift, what does Shana know? On and on. Everyone wants to know when and why Callen was tagged and tracked."

Dane tugged his phone out of his pocket. "I want some answers and soon. But first I have to find Shana."

Dane spent the next few hours frantically looking for Shana. She was nowhere to be found. She should have been on duty at the hospital today. She was a nurse there while Dane was an emergency room doctor. They had been raised together by their mother who came from a long line of healers within the shifter lineage. He and Shana had inherited their desire and ability to heal from her. They were among a number of shifters who worked at the hospital.

After checking the hospital, Shana's house and driving around town to see if he could find her, Dane stopped by her friend Phoebe's house.

Phoebe opened the door, her dark brown eyes wide with fear and worry. Phoebe was full human, a distant cousin to a shifter family. She was like a sister to him and fiercely protective of her shifter family and friends. Her dark hair was piled in a messy bun.

Before he could get a word out, Phoebe grabbed his arm and tugged him inside.

"I've been looking all over for Shana. I finally came home thinking maybe she stopped by. Have you seen her?" she asked.

The knot in Dane's stomach tightened. "You and me both. I was hoping you might know where she is. Have you heard the news?"

Phoebe nodded, tears filling her eyes. "Callen died on that highway in Connecticut. I think Shana must have heard the news on the way in to work. You have to find her, Dane!"

He nodded. "I know. Has she mentioned anything to you about Callen the last few weeks?"

"Just that she was worried about him because he was trying to confirm if there were shifters out West. She was afraid he might reveal himself somewhere unsafe and get killed. That's all she's mentioned out of the ordinary."

Dane sighed and ran a hand through his hair.

"Dammit, what the hell was going on with Callen? It makes no sense that he didn't shift back. I have a bad feeling about this. How the hell did he end up tagged?"

Phoebe stared back at him, fear flickering in her eyes. She gestured weakly, palms up in question, as she shook her head. Dane glanced at his watch. "I'm headed into the mountains. I'm guessing Shana took off to one of her hiding spots. Do you have to work tonight?"

Phoebe shook her head, and he continued. "Do you mind sitting tight? If I miss her out there, she'll probably come here when she gets back to town."

"No problem. I'll be here all night. Can you call me if you find her?"

"You got it."

Dane took off, calling Jake on the way to update him. He parked at one of the trailheads that intersected with the Appalachian Trail and started off on a solitary hike. It was late afternoon, and he needed to find a place to shift soon. He'd cover ground much faster in mountain lion form. He scrambled up a steep portion of the trail and cut off into the deep brush. In a flash, he shifted, his clothes falling, fur unfurling in a wave with a final twist when his body shifted fluidly into cat form. He moved swiftly and quietly, avoiding areas close to the heavily traveled Appalachian Trail. Unbeknownst to humans, the Appalachian Trail formed centuries ago as mountain lions stayed deep in the mountainous terrain and pushed north while humans sprawled forth into their territory. The trail ended in Maine beyond Catamount on Mount Katahdin—the area where the first litter of shifters was born. The litter's mother had moved slightly south when winter fell, just outside of Catamount, which at the time had been a nameless settlement in the late seventeenth century. The town was now mid-sized and bustling. Yet it lay close to the wilderness where mountain lions could shift and experience the freedom and solitude they craved.

Dane was running quietly along a ridge when he heard voices. He froze in place and backed up. Mountain lions were believed extinct in the East. Rumors abounded on alleged sightings, most true. Yet shifters tried to limit their exposure, preferring to keep the idea of mountain lions as ancient myth and long-gone from the forests of the east. It was safer that way. Callen's tragic death illuminated the dangers they faced. Though Dane wouldn't face that particular danger deep in the Maine woods, hunters were always a threat even though the species was protected.

He watched while a small group of hikers walked by. Quiet fell and then a lone woman emerged on the trail. He was positioned on a steep hill, hidden amongst the trees. He could see her clearly. She was so beautiful it took his breath away. She had honey blonde hair falling in loose waves around her shoulders. Her build was strong and curvaceous. A tank top pulled tightly across her breasts and jean shorts rode up her thighs. He was so drawn to her he had to force himself to be still. The task was made much more difficult in his cat form. As a cat, he was driven by instinct and primal urges. And whoever this woman was, she called to every cell in his body. He made himself wait longer than necessary after she passed by, so he could manage the strength of pull he felt for her.

The light faded and a storm rolled in. Dane had yet to find Shana when he was forced to find shelter from the storm himself. As he approached one of his preferred caves, he saw a human form limping along the faint trail leading to the cave and stumble inside. He thought it was the woman he saw earlier. She looked hurt. He stopped in his tracks. His concern for her ran so deep it was visceral. He slipped under the boughs of a balsam tree and waited.

When it was almost dark, he shifted back into human form. Before heading to the cave, he quickly checked for one of the small packs he kept hidden among rocks nearby. Such packs were well hidden and scattered for miles in these woods for shifters to have quick access to clothing and human supplies if they needed to shift into human form unexpectedly. He dressed, slung the pack over his shoulder and walked to the cave. The woman was asleep on the ground. She was inside a sleeping bag, but shivering visibly. Dane approached her slowly, touching her on the shoulder. Her eyes flew open. In the faded light, her soft green eyes shone through, filled with fear.

Dane held his hands up. "Hey, it's okay. I got caught in the storm too. Looks like we had the same idea. Are you okay?"

His pulse had skyrocketed the moment she opened her eyes and he got a good look at her face. He could look into her eyes all day—mossy, forest green and lush. Her mouth was full and sensual. Those eyes and her honey brown hair brought to mind a warm summer day.

She pushed herself up to a seated position, a grimace flashing across her face.

"Are you hurt?" His protective instincts ran high. A side effect of developing the capacity to shift was that mountain lions with this ability were intensely protective of those they cared about. The solitary behavior of mountain lions in the wild was curbed out of self-preservation. To save each other and the species, they had to develop the capacity to watch after each other. This woman, whoever she was, was so compelling, Dane only wanted to wrap her in his arms and keep her safe. Along with a few other things, but that wasn't his focus now since she looked close to hypothermia and injured.

She stared at him and seemed to conclude he meant

her no harm. "I slipped on some wet rocks. I sprained my ankle and scraped my leg pretty bad. I can't believe I fell. I'm almost to the end of the trail. I made it all the way from Georgia without getting hurt."

Dane forced himself to focus, pulled his backpack off and reached inside for the small medical kit he kept in every pack he stashed. "I'm Dane Ashworth, by the way."

"I'm Chloe, Chloe Silver," she replied quietly.

"So how long have you been on the trail?" he asked as he pulled out antiseptic, ointment and bandages.

"Almost six months. I started in mid-May."

He nodded, realizing he needed some light to help with her injuries. "Hang on." He stood and strode towards the back of the cave, trying to make it look as if he was peering around when he knew precisely where he kept a pile of dry wood in the back of the cave.

"What are you doing?" Chloe asked.

"Seeing if there's any wood in here." He returned with a pile of sticks and quickly laid them over the blackened area where he'd previously had fires. Her shivering hadn't stopped. Hypothermia was a real danger in this weather. He needed the light and a fire would help keep them warm.

In short order, he had a fire started and heat started to circle in the small cave.

"Can I see your leg?"

She hesitated and then shrugged. She shimmied out of her sleeping bag. Dane's heart clenched at the sight of her leg. Her ankle was swollen, and the side of the same leg was scraped from thigh to ankle. The skin was red and swollen, particularly on her thigh.

"You weren't kidding, you have some bad scrapes there. Where do you want me to start? I'd prefer to stabilize your ankle first."

Chloe's green eyes widened. "Wouldn't it be best if a doctor did that? I'm sure we can make it through the night and get help in the morning."

Dane grinned. "I am a doctor," he said simply.

"Oh…oh. Well, in that case, I guess do whatever you think we need to do. The sooner the better, right?"

He nodded firmly. "Definitely. He dug through his kit to see if he had anything firm to help hold her ankle in place. "Give me a sec."

A short while later, Chloe's ankle was stabilized. Dane had used cotton bandaging to hold it in place. He was relieved it appeared to be a bad sprain, but she hadn't broken it. She'd been a trooper through the whole thing. She now sat quietly while he swabbed the scrapes on her leg with alcohol, dabbing them with an ointment quickly. The only sign of her pain was when her breath hissed through her teeth.

Satisfied he'd done all he could, Dane carefully placed gauze over the scrapes. He tugged his water bottle out and handed it to her with some ibuprofen. "This will take the edge off the pain."

Chloe's smile was tired, but she took the water and ibuprofen. Dane tugged his own sleeping bag out and laid it beside hers. "I know we just met and we're in a cave in the middle of the woods, but it's cold and wet. I'm thinking it's best if we stay close to keep warm." Though his body wanted to be close to her for other reasons, he was speaking the truth.

Chloe's exhaustion was showing. Dane helped her carefully slide back into her sleeping bag. After she finally fell asleep, he lay down beside her, watching her sleep in the glow from the fire and wondering how he could show her who and what he was. The lion in him was drawn to her so strongly, he had to force himself to think rationally. If his cat had full say in the matter, he'd skip the preliminaries and make sure she understood she was the mate for him. But…his human side knew that was half-crazy no matter how much she called to him. Her flashing green eyes, her sensual curves and her steely strength were everything he wanted. He just had to find a way to show himself without scaring her. His worries about Shana flickered in the back of his mind. He knew she could take care of herself, but it didn't change the fear and worry clenching his gut. The loss of Callen could crush her. Behind that lay Dane's fear around what led Callen to his death.

Chapter 2

Chloe came awake slowly, savoring the warmth curled around her. She shifted her hips back, her bottom rubbing against what was most definitely an aroused man. The haze of sleep cleared. Opening her eyes, she saw the rock walls of the cave she'd found late yesterday evening after the storm rolled in. She remembered Dane and realized he was the warm, strong, intensely arousing man curled up behind her. When he'd woken her in the almost-dark, she'd been startled and a little fearful, but after only a few minutes, her gut told her he was completely trustworthy.

Though she'd been in pain last night, her body had reacted strongly to his presence. Not to mention that he was more than a tad easy on the eyes. He was tall, lean and strong. His golden brown hair had shone in the soft firelight, his blue-gray eyes were focused and intent. Every time he met her eyes, her belly fluttered. His steady presence while he efficiently bandaged her ankle and leg had made her feel safe and protected.

After stumbling into the cave, tired, afraid and in

pain, falling asleep with Dane at her side had been a haven. She couldn't help the fingers of desire that crept along her skin, but she barely knew him. Wondering if he was awake, she started to roll over only to gasp in pain. She'd forgotten to keep her ankle still.

Dane's hand came across her hips carefully and held her steady. "Easy. Don't move too fast." His voice was low and warm, caressing her nerves.

Heat slid through her, moisture building in her core. She wanted this man, who she barely knew, with a ferocity she'd never experienced. The depth of her longing was so intense it sent her pulse racing and a curl of fear through her veins. She forced herself to breath slowly. "I forgot about my ankle," Chloe said.

"Not a surprise," Dane replied, his voice husky from sleep. "Glad you slept deep enough to forget. I was worried you might have trouble sleeping between your fall and the bad weather."

Chloe smiled softly. She loved hearing he'd been worried about her. "I'm amazed I slept as well as I did. I think it's probably thanks to you." She carefully shifted to lie on her back, so she could see his face. She hadn't slept beside a man in over a year, so she felt a little awkward, the feeling magnified by the fact that she'd only met Dane last night under less than usual circumstances. When she turned over, he adjusted slightly, but didn't move his hand away from her hip.

He was resting on one elbow. His eyes skated over her body, a look of concern in them.

"I'm okay, better than I expected really," she said. Looking at him in the daylight sent her pulse skittering beyond control. Sun filtered through the opening of the cave, sparking gold in his hair. His blue-gray eyes were soft and intense. His features were sculpted, almost cat-like with his eyes tipped up at the corners. His lips were full and lush. His body had a coiled energy though he rested at her side, appearing completely at ease. She took advantage of the few seconds when he glanced away and allowed her eyes to dip below his face. He wore a faded blue t-shirt that clung to his muscles. Her hands itched to touch him. She wondered if she'd completely lost her mind. She was in a cave in the middle of the woods in Maine thinking about running her hands all over Dane's body, wet at the mere thought of his hard cock against her hip moments ago, and imagining what it would be like to act on her body's desire.

Dane turned back, his eyes colliding with hers. Chloe couldn't look away. He shifted his weight, never breaking eye contact. Desire shimmered in the air around them.

He finally spoke. "I hope this doesn't sound crazy, but I want to kiss you." He paused, his eyes searching her face. "Just tell me no, and this conversation never happened," he said gruffly, his eyes never breaking from hers.

Chloe wanted to kiss him more than she'd ever wanted anything. The fact that he asked, his polite words belying the fierce attraction she felt between them and the look in his eyes, made her want to kiss him even more. The pull was so strong it almost overpowered her. The sensible part of her, the part that had kept charge of her life and her heart for the last year after the bitter end of a relationship, had no say in this moment. Chloe lifted a hand and stroked it down his cheek. "I don't want to say no," she said softly.

Dane kept his eyes trained on hers as he leaned toward her. His lips landed against hers soft and sure. Time suspended. Dane kissed her as she'd never been kissed before. He began a slow, searing exploration of her lips with soft kisses and nips. He traced her mouth with his tongue. She opened, desperate for deeper contact with him. His tongue stroked inside—slow, patient and oh-so-thorough. Chloe tumbled into sensation, straining toward him. Wildness built within as their tongues tangled.

Dane's hand slid slowly up her hips, coasting across her abdomen, caressing its soft curve, before curling around one breast and then the other, his touch soft and tantalizing. She became frantic to be closer, to ease the ache building inside of her. He cupped her cheek, his thumb caressing where her pulse beat, and slowly pulled back.

She could have happily lost herself in his blue-gray gaze. He looked at her for a long moment, his eyes intense. "I want you more than I've ever wanted anyone," he said baldly, his voice low and clear. "And that's why we have to stop. Any more and I won't be able to stop."

Her breath hitched. Her pulse pounded under the soft caress of his thumb. Yearning coursed through her. She wanted to beg him to do anything other than stop. *Seriously, you're out of your mind. You barely know this guy. In fact, you met him in a cave in the dark. He's being sensible, points for him. You need to be sensible too.*

She nodded, biting her lip.

She saw his eyes darken, but he didn't move. "What would you say if I asked you to stay in Catamount for a few weeks?" he asked.

Chloe didn't hesitate. "Yes," she said simply. Reason began to filter in. "Are you hiking the trail too?"

Dane shook his head. "I live nearby in Catamount. I hike around here all the time. You're not going to be able to hike out with your ankle. You can come to my office, so I can do a better job of stabilizing your ankle. I made do last night, but I can do better with more than my emergency medical kit. You're welcome to stay with at my place, but if you're not sure about that, I can make other arrangements for you."

Chloe knew he was right. There was absolutely no way she would be able to finish the trail now. It was almost November. She was later than she'd wanted to be getting to the end of the trail. By the time her ankle could handle hiking again, winter would be here. "How am I even going to get to the closest trailhead like this?" she asked, gesturing to her ankle.

"I'll carry you," Dane said simply. "It's not that far. I hike around here a lot. I know a shortcut back to the closest trailhead." He paused, appearing to think. "I was out here looking for my sister yesterday. I need to see if I can find her."

"Is she lost or something?" Chloe asked, her curiosity deepening when she sensed Dane was holding something back.

Dane shook his head slowly. His hand still cupped her cheek, his thumb idly caressing her neck. His touch sent shivers all through her body. He looked at her intently, searching her eyes. He finally replied. "Shana loves to hike and comes here a lot. I couldn't find her yesterday, so I came to check on her. I've got one last spot to check where she might be camped. Do you mind waiting a little bit? I'll check and come right back."

Chloe couldn't have said no to him. His amazing eyes held a silent entreaty. The connection to him was unlike anything she'd ever experienced. Against all reason, she completely trusted him. "I'll wait for you. It's not like I'm going anywhere on my own," she said wryly.

Dane chuckled softly, his eyes sobering quickly. "Thank you," he said simply. He leaned forward, his lips coming against hers again. In a flash, sensation overtook her. He made her feel as if she was the center of the universe. He pulled away, swearing softly.

Protected Mate (Catamount Lion Shifters)

"I can't think straight when I'm near you," he said, carefully moving away from her, his hand coasting softly across her hips as he did.

Chloe's face was hot. She felt so flustered she didn't know what to say. She certainly couldn't think straight. Her brain was doing cartwheels over Dane's comment. He was like a magnet for her, so much so that her usual tendency to be reserved and hold back had dissolved under the force of attraction she felt. To hear he might be even remotely as unsettled as her ratcheted the thrum of desire inside. Dane didn't appear to expect her to say anything. He stood and stretched, walking to the entrance of the cave to look outside.

"Do you want me to help you get situated outside while I go see if Shana's camped up ahead?" he asked. "You'll be warmer in the sun."

"That'd be nice. How long will you be?"

"Maybe a half hour." He grabbed his backpack and walked outside.

Chloe tried to get up on her own, wanting to follow him outside and quickly realized her body had quite a bit to say about that. Dane returned just as she gasped in pain. The scraped area on her leg was incredibly sore while her ankle wanted nothing to do with any kind of motion.

He raced to her side. "Take it easy." He glanced over her quickly. "Can you wait a minute while I set up a spot where you can be comfortable while you wait?"

Chloe nodded, smiling ruefully. "I'm not the best patient."

He grinned. "I can see that. Be right back."

Moments later, he returned again. She'd propped herself up to sit with her back against the rock wall. Dane knelt beside her. Without a word, he slid an arm under her knees and the other under her hips, lifting her effortlessly.

He carefully set her down on his sleeping bag, which he'd situated on the ground by a large boulder she could lean against. He'd set a water bottle nearby. The area faced a beautiful valley with a stream running through the center of a small clearing.

"This is beautiful," she said with a sigh.

He stood. "I won't be long." He caught her eyes before he turned away. In that brief glance, Chloe's pulse ricocheted and she flushed.

"Okay. I'll be right here." Flutters danced in her belly and a smile warmed her inside and out.

Dane started off along a faint trail that followed the upper ridge along the hillside. His stride was long and loose. He disappeared into the trees. Chloe rested against the boulder. Birds chattered nearby.

Sometime later, she heard a squawking in the field below and shaded her eyes to look. There was a cluster of turkeys in the valley. She'd heard wild turkeys had been reintroduced up here. As she watched, she caught her breath. A mountain lion walked casually through the valley. The animal was a large, tawny cat, lean and muscled. The lion ignored the turkeys and paused to drink from the stream. Another mountain lion, smaller and slighter, appeared behind it and waited nearby. Chloe was in awe. She'd heard there were reports of mountain lions still roaming wild in this area, but they'd been declared extinct in the eastern United States for years. As the cats disappeared into the trees on the far side of the valley, she let her breath out. She realized perhaps she should be afraid, but they were so beautiful, she was in awe.

Checking her watch, she wondered when Dane would return. As if she'd conjured him by thought, he strode back into the small clearing where she sat, a woman she presumed to be his sister with him. His sister shared his striking looks. Though not as tall, she was fit and muscular, her build softened with curves. Her hair was the same tawny golden brown shade and hung in loose waves around her shoulders. Her eyes were gray and intent and held a sadness within.

"Hey there," Chloe said with a smile, uncertain how to explain her presence.

Dane smiled when he met her eyes. Just a glance and electricity arced between them. "Chloe, this is Shana, my sister," he said, gesturing to Shana. He looked back to Shana. "Like I said, I found Chloe last night when I was looking for you. She sprained her ankle on the trail and holed up in this cave when it started raining yesterday evening."

Shana nodded politely though she didn't smile. "Nice to meet you. I'm glad Dane found you. I hear you're stopping in Catamount for a bit." Her words were gracious though devoid of any warmth, flat almost.

Chloe didn't know what was wrong, but she sensed a deep sadness from Shana. Realizing now wasn't the time or place to try to figure that out, she nodded. "I can't really finish the Appalachian Trail with a sprained ankle. Dane suggested I stop for a little while. I'll have to figure out what I'm doing next anyway."

Shana nodded and looked to Dane. "Want me to carry the packs, so you can carry Chloe?" She asked this as if it was a completely common occurrence for Dane to carry a woman out of the woods.

At Dane's nod, Shana efficiently set to work getting the packs ready to go. Chloe had no idea how she'd manage, but Shana effortlessly lifted Chloe's pack, along with Dane's and lashed them together on her back. Dane lifted Chloe into his arms, and followed Shana down the trail. Shana's silence was weighted, and Dane was subdued around her. Doubts crept into her thoughts as Dane carried her through the dappled light of the forest.

Chapter 3

Dane pulled up at his office and turned to Chloe in the passenger seat. He'd dropped Shana off at Phoebe's house a few minutes earlier. Chloe had been quiet on the drive down from the trail. Weariness edged her features. Her mossy green eyes met his, and she smiled hesitantly. "Is this your office?"

"Yup. I'd like to get a better look at your ankle as soon as possible." He climbed out of the truck and went around to her side. She'd already started to get out. "I can tell you're not the best patient," he said with a chuckle.

She grinned in reply, her eyes lighting up. He could look in her eyes all day and never tire of it. They were soothing and electrifying at once.

"I'm terrible at resting, but I'll try to be good," she said, brushing a few loose tendrils of hair out of her eyes.

Before she could argue, he lifted her out of the car, adjusted her in his arms and carried her inside.

"Dane! You don't have to carry me everywhere. I can lean on your arm and hobble in."

"Not until I get a look at your ankle when I have

some decent light. I'm confident it'll be okay, but we need it to be more stable." He refrained from telling her he loved having an excuse to touch her and that the feel of her lush curves in his arms was heaven.

A while later, she walked out beside him, only partly resting her weight on his arm. He'd put an air brace on her ankle and thoroughly cleaned the scrapes on her leg. She was going to be fine, but it would be a few weeks at least before she could put her full weight on her ankle. He fervently hoped she'd stay in Catamount long enough for him to persuade her... *Persuade her to do what? Have you lost your mind? Your lion thinks he's found his mate, but don't be stupid. You're a shifter, and she has no clue. None. Slow down and be rational about this.*

Dane's internal conversation was a reflection of who and what he was—half human and half mountain lion. His human side was the voice of reason while his lion side was driven by primal instinct. And he wanted Chloe... fiercely. He'd tried to talk her into staying with him, but she seemed too hesitant, so he'd improvised and made arrangements for her to stay at a local inn. She'd agreed to lunch with him after she checked in and tolerated him lugging her backpack into the room for her.

A while later, he walked slowly at her side into The Trailhead Café, a local favorite. The café served a mix of diner basics with creative, healthy fare. It was housed in an old-style diner building with shiny stainless, polished steel on the outside and a bright red roof. Inside the café had a counter with an exposed kitchen and booths lining the walls. The walls were plastered with photos of through-hikers of the Appalachian Trail and faded newspaper photos of mountain lions. Many, but not all, of the locals knew the mountain lions weren't a myth. The locals who knew the truth protected the shifters by perpetuating the myth for tourists.

Dane contemplated how and when he could reveal himself to Chloe. This was something he'd never needed to do. The women he'd been involved with before were either shifters themselves, or women who knew what shifters were and weren't intimidated. He couldn't know if she'd be frightened or disgusted. Or worse, not believe him at all. He could easily show her the truth, but he didn't want to shift into a wild animal without her at least being partially open to the concept. Mountain lion shifters had mated with humans over centuries. He knew it was entirely possible and yet there were plenty of obstacles. The first being how and when to reveal himself. He didn't want to contemplate what it would mean if she refused to accept him as he was. For now, he wanted to enjoy lunch with her. Not long after they were seated, Jake came in and walked straight to their table.

"Hey, saw your truck outside," Jake said by way of greeting. His eyes were puzzled when he glanced at Chloe.

"Hey Jake, this is Chloe. Ran into her last night when I was out looking for Shana. She's a through-hiker, but as you can see, she sprained her ankle. She'll be in town for a little bit." He had more questions than he could count about Chloe, realizing he'd just given Jake almost all of the information he had about her. Against all reason, he was convinced she was the woman for him and yet he knew next to nothing about her.

Chloe smiled politely at Jake. She'd showered and changed at the hotel while he waited outside. Her honey blonde hair fell in loose waves around her shoulders, her green eyes bright. She stuck her booted foot out from under the table. "Dane bandaged my ankle and put a brace on it today. I won't be able to finish the trail, but there's not much I can do about that."

Jake's eyes held a glimpse of heat. Dane's cat bristled inside. Jake must have sensed it because he shuttered his eyes and looked back at Dane. With a barely perceptible wink, he asked, "Any news?"

Dane shook his head. "Nope. Found Shana this morning. She'd gone to one of her favorite spots last night." He paused as he considered how to explain Shana's situation to Chloe and elected to hew as close to the truth as he could.

"Shana's husband died in a car accident the other day. She loves to hike, but I got worried yesterday when she wasn't back by afternoon. That's why I went looking for her and ended up finding you," Dane said, looking to Chloe.

"Oh I'm so sorry!" Chloe replied, her hand coming to her chest. "I thought she looked sad today, but I had no idea. Obviously."

"Of course not," Dane said. He glanced back to Jake. "Any news on your end?"

Jake shrugged. "Not much. I'll let you know if I hear anything. How's Shana?"

Dane sighed. "I think she hasn't really absorbed it yet. I'm worried about her, but she's not talking much right now. She asked me to take her to Phoebe's, so that's where she is right now. She doesn't want to go home. Says it will just make her think of Callen. I'm heading over to her house tomorrow to get some things packed for her. Do you want to meet me there? I could use a little help." He hoped to do some searching on Callen's computer and see what he could find. Jake was a computer programmer. With Jake's help, he'd get further than he would on his own. He'd known Callen was trying to confirm the rumors about mountain lion shifters in the Midwest, but Callen tended to play his cards close. Dane couldn't shake the feeling that someone had set out to kill Callen. Shana shared his concern, but she didn't have it in her right now to look into it. She was in shock and grieving.

Jake nodded. "You got it. Just give me a call." Jake turned to Chloe. "Nice to meet you. Hope you enjoy your stay here." With that, he turned and left.

Once their food was ordered, Dane looked across the table at Chloe. "So what made you decide to hike the Appalachian Trail?"

Chloe tilted her head and remained quiet for a moment. "Not to sound corny, but I needed to challenge myself. My dad used to take me hiking all the time when I was a kid. He died a few years back, and when life... happened, I decided a good, long hike might help me get back on track."

Chloe's eyes clouded while she spoke. He sensed there was far more to the story. "Life happened?"

Chloe bit her lip, making Dane desperately want to kiss her again. He forced himself to stay focused. She sighed and shrugged. "I've told half the hikers I met on the trail my story, no reason not to tell you." She looked up with a tired smile. "It's funny on the trail. Everyone has a story of why they're hiking over two thousand miles and usually it's something that has nothing to do with hiking. For me, I thought I did everything right up until a year ago. I was the good girl—straight A student, graduated from high school and then college with honors, got engaged to my college sweetheart and so on." She paused and took a sip of water, bitterness followed by sadness flashing through her eyes. "I found out my fiancée had been screwing around on me the whole time we were dating. It was kind of an accident that I even found out. I used to manage a clothing store and a woman he was dating on the side shopped there. Anyway, she showed me a picture on

her phone—of her boyfriend who happened to be my
fiancée. She had no idea who I was."

A fierce, primal flash of anger raced through him.
He had to beat back the cat in him, which rose to the
surface when he was angry. He schooled his expression to
calm and glanced out the window for a moment, needing to
gather himself. Reined in, he turned back to her. "Chloe, I
can't believe you had to go through that…"

Chloe shook her head quickly. "It's okay. It was
awful, but I'm glad I found out before we got married. I
was just kind of going along in life. I thought if I did
everything I was supposed to, I would be happy. Even
before that, I wasn't. So yeah, it sucked and it hurt like hell.
But in the end, it was for the best. I'd gotten a business
degree and was bored out of my mind trying a run a store
where I had no say in what we sold. I quit, took my savings
and planned this hike. Here I am," she said with a grin.

Dane wanted to find her former fiancée and punch
him. How could anyone not realize how amazing she was?
But then, he supposed perhaps he should thank the guy. If
he hadn't been such an idiot, Dane might never have met
Chloe. "And so now that you've hiked all the way to
Maine, what's next?"

Chloe grinned sheepishly and glanced up as their
waiter approached the table. After the waiter set their
sandwiches down in front of them and filled their drinks,
Dane waited while Chloe took a bite of her sandwich. "Oh
wow, this is so good!"

Dane chuckled. "Yeah, the Trailhead knows how to
make a good sandwich."

Chloe nodded vigorously. "I mean, this is gourmet
—in the middle of Maine." She'd ordered a Portobello
mushroom sandwich with sundried tomatoes and a spicy
aioli spread.

"Maine's got amazing food. Have you been to Portland?"

Chloe shook her head as she took another bite of her sandwich.

"Portland's the 'new' New York City when it comes to restaurants. Big on the whole fresh, organic, locally sourced kinds of food. It's not too far from here. We could head down for a day or two," Dane said with a smile, realizing that might be a perfect way to have a few days to himself with Chloe.

Chloe took another few bites as she nodded before finally pausing for a breath.

"So back to you, what were you planning to do when you finished the trail?" Dane asked.

Chloe shrugged. "That's the thing, I purposefully didn't make any plans. I've always been a planner. I planned every step of my life up until I broke up with Tom. Look where it got me? In a job that bored me silly about to marry a man who'd spent most of our relationship with other women on the side."

"So you're almost done with the trail, you sprained your ankle and the snow's about to fly any day now?"

Chloe nodded and grinned. "I guess so. I have some savings left. Being a planner, I had a nice little bundle saved up. Hiking is pretty cheap, so I've spent hardly anything. For now, I'm planning to enjoy lunch with you and see what happens next."

Dane looked across the table at her, his eyes locking onto hers. Heat sizzled between them. He didn't want to scare her, but he wanted her more than he'd ever wanted anyone. He'd found her and wasn't planning to let go. The wheels in his mind turned as he contemplated how to convince her Catamount was the perfect place for her...and that she was meant to be his mate. The human half of his brain kicked in. *Seriously? Your cat thinks this is meant to be, but that's all primal instinct and testosterone. Slow down. You don't even know if she can accept who you are. Let's take this one step at a time.*

Dane forced his eyes away again, following the path of a leaf twisting on the breeze as it drifted to the ground. Right, one step at a time. Easier said than done when lust streaked through him every second he was with her.

Chapter 4

Chloe sat down on her hotel bed and looked around the room. The inn where Dane had brought her was cozy and luxurious. He'd refused to let her pay. After almost six months of hiking and camping, the quick hot shower she'd taken earlier had been sheer heaven. She decided a bath was in order. Dane had shown her how to remove the air brace, so she carefully removed it while waiting for the tub to fill. The scrapes on her leg were sore, but she was tired, worn out and wanted the comfort of a long bath.

Dane's questions about her plans had made her wonder what she was going to do. She'd been truthful when she'd told him she didn't have any plans, but now that she was face to face with what it meant, part of her was terrified. She'd hoped the sense of accomplishment she felt from finishing the Appalachian Trail would buoy her onto whatever would happen next in her life. Somehow, ending her hike with a sprained ankle fizzled those dreams. Strangely though, she felt a sense of fate when Dane had found her in the cave last night.

When he'd told her he wanted to kiss her, Chloe's

heart beat to the resonance he evoked. And then there was the kiss, which pretty much blew her mind. She couldn't even think about it without blushing, and all they'd done was kiss. With a shake of her head, she stood and limped to the bathroom.

Moments later, she carefully climbed into the tub, keeping her ankle propped up on the side. The hot water relaxed her. Resting her head against the edge of the tub, Dane filled her thoughts. When she was near him, there was a constant current between them. It went beyond mere attraction. After her engagement was in shambles, Chloe had wondered if she'd ever trust again. Though her mind resisted, her heart completely trusted Dane. And if her body had any say in the matter, well, she'd never have hesitated at his offer to stay with him. Her mind had to raise its voice to be heard in that little internal disagreement. Just thinking about his smoky blue-gray eyes and the feel of his lips on hers and heat unfurled in her body. Her hand unconsciously toyed with her nipples, imagining Dane's hands there.

The aftermath of her engagement falling apart and months of hiking had taken her to a chaste place, which she'd needed for a while. But now, Dane's touch had flicked a switch. She was hot and bothered—all by herself in the bathtub. She slid a hand down her abdomen and into her moist folds. She was swollen with desire. Teasing herself, all she could think about was Dane. She abruptly sat up. She was so close to the edge, but she didn't want to tumble over by herself.

Swearing at how slowly she had to move, she got out of the tub and dried off. Tugging her phone out of her purse, she opened her contacts. She'd added Dane's number earlier today after he dropped her off.

Swatting her rational thoughts away, she called him. He picked up on the second ring.

"Hey Chloe, is everything okay?"

The sound of his low voice amped up the desire humming through her. "I want to see you," she said, her voice raspy.

"Give me ten minutes and I'll be there," Dane said swiftly. Before she could reply, he hung up.

She sat on the bed wondering what the hell she was thinking. She'd met him in the dark in a cave in the middle of the woods. She knew almost nothing about him, other than that he was a doctor, he had a sister, and he lived in Catamount. Everything she felt didn't make sense. She felt as if she'd known him for years. Her heart hammered against her ribs, anticipation fluttering in her veins.

***

Dane careened down the hill toward town where Chloe was staying. Her voice had set him on fire. After lunch, he'd reluctantly dropped her off at the inn and returned to his office. He'd spent the next few hours doing some online digging with Jake's help. He didn't like prying into Callen's email accounts after he died, but he had a suspicion if there were any clues that might tell him why Callen was in mountain lion form weeks after he'd flown out West, they might be there. Callen had been one of the alphas in their mountain lion clan, his family along with Dane's and two others the founding families of Catamount, the name selected because it was an old nickname for mountain lions.

Centuries ago, the dwindling mountain lions in the eastern United States kept pushing further north as humans spread into their territory. During this precarious time, litters of mountain lions began to be born with the ability to shift from cat to human. This became their last line of defense against extinction. Before mountain lions became shifters to save themselves, they'd had a loose hierarchy with alphas claiming the broadest swathes of territory, but otherwise living solitary lives. After being driven to smaller and smaller corners of the wilderness and developing the ability to shift, alphas functioned more as leaders among their clans and were fiercely protective of their families.

For as long as eastern mountain lions had been shifters, rumors had swirled there were shifters in other parts of the country. Though the West had bigger populations of wild mountain lions, it was rumored they were so established because there were hidden shifters among them. Callen had been determined to find them. He reasoned the eastern species needed to grow and wanted to connect with their counterparts elsewhere. Dane, just as alpha as Callen but less interested in throwing his weight around, had disagreed and repeatedly shared his concern that Callen was risking their safety with his research. After plowing through way too many emails, he and Jake had flagged a series of emails with a man who worked for the United States Fish and Wildlife Service and lived in Montana. Dane's stomach churned with worry that Callen may have accidentally revealed their presence to the government.

The potential ramifications of that were disastrous. As it was, mountain lions were relegated to mere fractions of the territory they once roamed. If the government discovered the existence of mountain lion shifters, they faced the threat of regulation, being fenced in, being forced to report their whereabouts, or even worse, being rounded up and studied. The possibilities were horrifying. Catamount shifters had protected their existence for centuries. The trait to shift from human to lion and back again was the key to their secret and to their safety. If Callen had put that at risk…the mere thought of it sickened

Dane. Jake had left moments before Chloe called, promising to get to work tomorrow and try to hack into the man's computer.

Chloe's voice had been music to Dane's ears. Not only did he want to get his mind off of his worries about what happened to Callen and what it meant for his kind, he desperately wanted every minute he could have with Chloe. He didn't know precisely why she'd called and so bluntly stated she wanted to see him, but he didn't even consider saying no.

He knocked quickly on her door. Chloe opened it, and Dane's blood heated at the sight of her. Her honey blonde hair was damp with soft tendrils framing her face. Her green eyes were bright. She was wearing nothing other than a robe. He swallowed at the realization that she was likely bare underneath it. Her skin was flushed.

"Hey," she said simply, her voice low and husky.

He stepped through the door. She remained standing just beyond where the door swung open. Realizing she couldn't move quickly because of her ankle, he moved out of the way and closed the door, never taking his eyes off of her.

"Hey," he returned, standing in front of her and brushing a loose lock of hair away from her cheek. A mere touch and lust streaked through him, his cat arching and stretching inside. He forced himself to hold still for a moment, trying to read her eyes. He saw vulnerability and uncertainty mixed with heat and desire. Her tongue darted out to lick her lips, and he was gone. "Tell me if this is too much," he whispered right before his lips came against hers.

Dane's blood pounded in his ears, desire thundering through him. Chloe's lips were soft and luscious. Her mouth opened instantly to his, her tongue tangling in a slow dance with his. He stepped closer, barely able to remember he needed to be careful of her ankle and leg. He slipped his arms around her, bringing her against his body. The feel of her curves against his hard muscles wiped his mind clear of all thought. Instinct driving him, he slid one hand slowly down her back to cup her bottom, so soft and round. His other hand traveled down her neck, coasting across her pulse and curling around her breast, so heavy and hot in his hand. A soft sound escaped her throat, and his cock pulsed against the cradle of her hips.

He forced himself to gentle his lips and still his hands. He was about to take her—right here, right now.

"Chloe," he whispered urgently.

She opened those green eyes, misty with desire. Her lips were swollen and she strained against him. Her breath was ragged. "I wanted to see you because I…" She paused, a flush washing her face. "I've never felt this way about anyone. I just needed to see you," she said simply. She broke away from his gaze, her eyes unfocused. She bit her lip.

"Don't be nervous," he said gruffly, sensing she was. "It's the same for me."

Her eyes flew back to his, a furrow forming between them. "It is?"

He nodded. He tried to think of how to slow this down and find a way to tell her what he was. His brain could barely function. When Chloe took a few steps back and untied her rode, letting it fall open, his knees buckled. He was lost.

"Before you got here, I couldn't stop thinking about you…" she whispered, lifting her hands to cup her breasts. "I decided I didn't want to be alone, to only think about you." Her eyes were bold and shy at once.

Dane took two strides, stopping abruptly inches

away from her. His entire body vibrated with need, the force so powerful, he could barely restrain it. He closed his eyes and took a shuddering breath. When he opened them, meeting her soft green gaze, her eyes intent on him, he had to shake his head to focus. "You have to know I want you more than I've wanted anyone ever. But I don't want to rush you..."

She placed her finger against his lips. "You're not rushing me. I'm rushing you. I can't not do this." She dropped her hand, eyes on him, expectant and waiting.

He let his forehead fall to hers. They stood like that for a long moment, time suspended, before he took her lips. An incremental step closer and he finally felt her soft curves against him. That itself was such heaven, the memory would stay with him for a lifetime.

***

Chloe thought for a moment Dane wouldn't give her what she wanted. She couldn't explain what she felt, only that she wasn't going to let her old, tired planning mind talk her out of this. Her body came to life like a tuning fork around Dane. Desire rushed through her in waves. All she wanted was to feel his bare skin against hers and to let the passion that sparked and flickered burst into flame.

He kissed her softly at first until she reached up and tugged him closer, stroking her tongue against his. Their kiss went wild, deep strokes, nips and nibbles. Their breath mingled in gasps. She pressed into his hard body, glorying in the feel of the planes of his muscled chest and abdomen against her breasts. Dane's lips left hers with a groan. His eyes pinned hers, the blue darker and deeper. He took a step back and carefully lifted her.

"We have to get you off your feet," he said, his

voice raspy.

In a few strides, he reached the bed and carefully set her down, tugging the pillows to prop behind her head. Her robe fell further open. She didn't know what had come over her, but she felt no modesty around him. She shifted her shoulders, and the robe fell away from her breasts.

Dane's breath hitched. "You have no idea what you do to me," he bit out.

"I want to feel you against me."

Dane tore his shirt off, revealing a chest that exceeded her fantasies. He was all muscle, lean and sinuous. He kicked his shoes off and carefully lowered himself on the bed beside her. The bed dipped with his weight, and she didn't resist the roll of her body right into his. The feel of his skin against hers was electric.

Dane closed his eyes and groaned, rolling to his side and lifting a hand to caress down her shoulder, curling around the curve of her breast, into the dip of her waist and coming to rest on the rise of her hip. He took a shuddering breath when she arched against him.

"Chloe…we have to slow down…" he rasped out.

"I just want to be close to you," she whispered.

It was the bare truth. A tiny corner of her mind tried to remind her that this was crazy. She'd been with only one man. Before she'd met Tom in college, her experience with men had been limited to a few kisses. She had lost her virginity to Tom and gone on to have several years of reliably mediocre sex, never even contemplating her body could feel the way it did when she simply got near Dane. She didn't know what was going to happen, but she wasn't going to deprive herself of the chance to feel something she'd never felt before.

She looked up at Dane's face. His hand was on her hip and her breasts grazed his chest. His eyes were closed, his breathing ragged. Wishing she could move more nimbly, Chloe pushed herself up and placed a hand on his chest. His eyes flew open, dark with desire. She leaned forward and brought her lips to his. The barest touch and he devoured her mouth. He shifted them so she was resting against the pillows again and proceeded to kiss her senseless. Deep, openmouthed, wild kisses.

Time dissolved into the curtain of passion that fell around them. Chloe succumbed to sensation, tumbling headfirst into the force that pulsed between them. Kisses moved from her lips down her neck to the tops of her breasts. He slowly pushed her robe back off her shoulders. She wore nothing other than a pair of practical cotton panties underneath. She'd wished she had something sexy to wear when she'd called Dane, but when she'd packed for this long hike, so many months ago, she'd been certain sexual encounters would not be on the list of her activities, so she packed only what she needed for months of hiking.

When Dane leaned up and trailed his fingers down between her breasts, over the soft curve of her belly to trace across the top of her panties, he smiled softly. "So sexy," he whispered.

"These?" she asked, gesturing to the white cotton panties.

"Yes, so practical and perfect. You don't need to do anything other than be you."

"Oh." She met his eyes and careened into the intensity of his gaze.

When he brought his lips to her body, he began a slow exploration that left her breathless, gasping and half out of her mind. He mapped her body with his lips and tongue, careful not to dislodge the bandages on her leg. His touch was light and sure at once. He stroked, licked and nipped. Her breasts were aching for more, and her desire built to a wet frenzy in her core. When he finally closed his lips over a nipple, she almost cried in relief. He proceeded to bring her higher and higher by teasing her nipples with suction, rolling the hard peaks between his fingers, and softly biting.

"Dane…" she gasped fitfully.

"I'm here."

"I…ahhh…need…"

"This?"

He asked just as he slid his fingers through her curls to stroke into her folds, which were drenched with her desire. Her hips bucked against his hand. Everything was a blur. His hard body beside hers, emanating heat and barely restrained lust. His fingers teased her, grazing over her clit, dipping into and out of her channel—over and over and over again. She teetered on the edge. Just when she thought she could bear no more, he drove two fingers in deeply, his thumb caressing her precisely where she needed it. Her climax ripped through her.

She floated down in a haze. Dane's hand stilled before he shifted and dragged it up to rest on the soft curve of her abdomen. He was leaning on his elbow, his eyes on her. His pulse beat rapidly in his neck. She lifted a hand— she could hardly believe she could move—and rested it against his chest to feel his heart thudding. He still wore his jeans.

Chloe wasn't sure what to say when he didn't move, remaining quiet and still at her side, his presence coiled and intent. She was still reeling from the most explosive orgasm she'd ever had and the one and only she'd had with anyone other than herself. She slipped her hand down his chest, coasting across the front of his jeans and curling around his hard shaft, heat emanating into her palm.

He swallowed and moved quickly, tugging her hand

away and lifting it. He turned it up and placed a soft kiss in her palm. The kiss was like a pebble dropped in water, the ripples starting in her center and reverberating throughout her body. "Not now," he said gruffly when she looked at him.

"But…"

He shook his head sharply. "This has already gone faster and farther than I intended." He paused, his eyes closing, as he took a deep breath. He appeared to be on the verge of physical pain. When he turned her palm, she idly stroked her thumb across his wrist and almost jumped when she felt his pulse pounding there.

Dane chuckled. "I want you," he said baldly, his blue-gray eyes intent. "More than I've ever wanted anyone. And that's why we're putting a pause on this. I'm not looking for a quick lay. I want much more than that."

Chloe took his words in. Though she appreciated his point, her body felt the pierce of disappointment. She wanted more…so much more. Her heart and body sang at his words, but she hadn't examined her feelings for Dane much. Frankly, the depth and intensity of them in such a short time should have sent alarm bells ringing. But something about Dane simply made her feel safe, protected…and more desired than she'd ever felt in her life. Not to mention, she was more drawn to him that she could even wrap her brain around as evidenced by the fact that she barely knew him and hadn't even thought twice about dropping her robe open and all but dragging him to bed with her.

She took a deep breath. "Well then."

When she looked up, he smiled, his eyes tipping at the corners, again reminding her of a cat.

Chapter 5

The next morning, Dane met Jake at Shana and Callen's house as planned to continue what they'd started yesterday and hopefully find more answers than questions. Dane got Jake set up on Callen's computer before getting started on packing for Shana. She'd texted him a short list of items she wanted. He quickly took care of it and loaded the boxes in his truck. Returning to the kitchen, he tugged a chair beside Jake where he sat at the table silently. Though Jake barely moved, he quickly flicked the mouse and scrolled through screens at a rapid pace. He had a flash drive plugged in to save whatever he found.

"Anything?" Dane asked.

About the only thing that kept his mind off Chloe were his worries about what happened to Callen. Though even with the looming fear around that, Chloe danced in the edges of his thoughts.

Jake made a few clicks before answering. "A few leads to chase. The guy that kept popping up in his email, Hayden Thorne, works for Fish and Wildlife. I can't pin anything on it, but he had a ton of contact with Callen recently, and all of it was about mountain lions and rumors about shifters. He made it sound like he was fascinated with the myth and all that, but he asked a lot of questions. Too many. And I hate that he works for the Feds."

"Yeah, that detail makes me more than a little nervous," Dane replied.

Jake saved whatever he was working on and ejected the flash drive, pocketing it quickly. He swiveled in the chair and looked at Dane. "So what's up with Chloe?"

Dane didn't even bother hiding it. Jake was a shifter too. He knew damn well what he sensed from Dane yesterday. "She's mine," he said simply before catching himself. "Let me rephrase, the cat in me would like to make her mine. But I have some sense, so I'm trying to figure out how the hell to tell her who and what I am."

Jake chuckled. "I gathered that's what you're hoping, but how serious are you?"

"More serious than I've ever been. As soon as I got near her, I knew she was the one."

Jake's grin faded, his blue eyes becoming thoughtful. "So when exactly do you plan to let her know you're a shifter? And what that even means?"

Dane rolled his head around, easing the tension in his neck. "As soon as I can. Just trying to figure out the how and when. I don't want to put it off. I can't have her thinking I tried to hide it from her. But damn if I know how to go about it. Any advice?"

Jake shook his head slowly. "You know how it went for me the one time I tried. Not good."

Jake had fallen in love with a woman in college. To this day, Dane didn't think it was love, but rather lust. But when Jake showed her who and what he was, she freaked out. The culmination being that she left campus never to been seen again, but not before she spread plenty of rumors and left the shifters busy debunking the rumor mill. Jake had sworn off any woman who wasn't a shifter since then, but that definitely limited options. There was also the fact that shifter clans stayed stronger and healthier if they expanded with humans. To find Chloe and feel the way he did with her, Dane didn't want to lose her. He couldn't shake the worry of how to tell her and what to do if it didn't go well.

Dane nodded. "I know. I'm hoping it won't go like that with Chloe." He ran his hands through his hair. "I'll figure it out."

***

Chloe walked slowly down the street perusing the various storefronts, carefully maneuvering with the air brace on her ankle. Catamount had a quintessential New England town green surrounded by small business housed in old classical structures. She'd fallen asleep in Dane's warm embrace last night to awaken alone. He'd sent a text in the early hours of the morning.

I'm headed home. I have a few things to do in the morning. Will see you later on.

Simply reading his words sent her heart racing. Dane triggered fantasies and hopes she'd never considered. After her abrupt disillusionment with men and life last year, she'd formed this idea she'd hike the Appalachian Trail and come out of it strong and independent, never feeling like she needed a man ever again. This encounter with Dane was so otherworldly and so unlike anything she'd ever experienced, she had no idea how to incorporate it into whatever vision she'd had for herself. Her body literally craved him to a degree she should have found frightening. And yet, there was that strange comfort she felt with him. As if she'd known him forever.

A cheerful sign on an old colonial home caught her eye—Roxanne's Country Store, We have Everything. Unable to resist exploring what 'everything' was, Chloe pushed through the door into a warm bustling space. She hadn't realized she was as chilled as she was until she stepped inside. The late fall air blew in with her. Meandering through the aisles, she found Roxanne's did have a bit of everything from groceries to hardware to gifts and odds and ends. There was a cluster of people on one side where there was a deli and coffee shop with small tables scattered nearby.

As she approached the area, she felt the eyes of many on her. She was nothing if not polite, so she smiled and nodded. A stocky woman with blonde hair coiled into a loose bun held in place with a pen stood behind the counter. "Hi there," the woman in question called out. "Just visiting?"

Chloe moved to stand by the counter. "Yup. I was hiking the trail and sprained my ankle two days ago," she said, gesturing to her booted foot.

The woman leaned across the counter to look. "You sure did. How did you get yourself off the trail?"

Chloe hesitated for a moment, unsure she could even say Dane's name without blushing. Several others turned to look at her curiously. "I, uh, ran into a man on the trail, Dane. He helped carry me out."

The woman behind the counter smiled widely. "You couldn't have found a better guy to run into. I bet he also took care of that ankle for you," she said with a wink.

Chloe blushed as she nodded.

The woman chuckled. "That's Dane. I'm Roxanne, by the way."

"Oh, is this your store? It's great! You do have a bit of everything."

Roxanne chuckled. "We try to."

Chloe couldn't help her curiosity about Dane. "How do you know Dane?"

"Hard not to know Dane if you live around here. His family's one of the oldest ones in town. He and his sister are the fourth generation in their family here. He's a good guy and damn good doctor. You're lucky you ran into him out there."

Chloe thought back to last night when she'd all but gone up in flames in his arms and considered that perhaps, she was lucky in ways Roxanne didn't have in mind. But she smiled and nodded. "How long have you lived in Catamount?"

Roxanne didn't hesitate. "Oh, I was born here, just like Dane. My grandfather started this store back when I was a baby. Named it after me from the start."

"Hey Roxanne, any news about Callen?" A man asked as he approached the counter from the front of the store.

Chloe turned to see Jake who she'd met with Dane when they were having lunch yesterday. His eyes landed on her, and he smiled politely. He was tall and lanky with golden brown hair and blue eyes that shared the same cat-like quality Dane's eyes had, titling at the corners.

"Not much. They ran another story about that mountain lion that got hit in Connecticut though," Roxanne replied.

Though Chloe had now known Roxanne for a total of roughly three minutes, she sensed Roxanne was trying to convey something to Jake. Her curiosity piqued, Chloe watched Jake.

His eyes flicked to Chloe and back to Roxanne before he nodded. "Oh right. Yeah, people are flipping out over that one. Don't know why they're so damn surprised.

My guess is mountain lions have traveled that far many times. Without something concrete like that tracking device to prove it, no one even thinks it's possible."

He turned to Chloe. "How's your ankle?"

"Pretty good, but then it's in this brace, so it's not like it can move much. I'm hobbling around okay though."

Jake nodded. "Glad you ran into Dane. Couldn't have happened upon a better guy after you got hurt out there."

Chloe nodded. "I know. I didn't want to need a doctor in the middle of the woods, but finding one was a definite plus."

Jake's blue eyes searched her face. "So how long do you plan to stay in Catamount?"

She thought for a moment, feeling several pairs of eyes turn to her at Jake's question. She had enough sense to know this was a small enough place that curiosity would run high about any newcomers. Though she couldn't say she knew how long she planned to stay, she knew with certainty she wanted to stay long enough to explore whatever lay between her and Dane. What that meant, she didn't know, but she wasn't walking away. She decided the truth would be the best answer.

"I don't know. But at the moment, I don't have any plans to leave," she replied simply.

Jake's brows rose, prompting her to explain further. "When I decided to hike the Appalachian Trail, I didn't have any plans for what I'd do when I finished. Now I'm here, so I figure I might as well stay a bit."

Jake nodded, a slow smile spreading on his face. "Okay then. Well, make sure Dane shows you around. Ask him to take you out to Shadow Rock. Tell him I told you to."

At that, he winked at her and turned to leave before

she had a chance to ask him what he meant. Chloe looked back at Roxanne who had a speculative gleam in her eyes.

Unlike Jake, Roxanne didn't bother with cryptic references. "So, Dane must like you then," she said with a grin.

Chloe blushed, hating for the thousandth time that she was a blusher. She couldn't hide what she felt. She held Roxanne's gaze and shrugged. "Maybe?"

Roxanne burst out laughing. "Oh dear, he absolutely likes you. Do as Jake says and ask him to take you to Shadow Rock."

"Where's Shadow Rock and why should I ask Dane to take me there?" Chloe's curiosity notched higher. It was clear they were trying to push her in a direction. She was uncertain about what they thought she needed to see...*or know*.

Roxanne's laugh quieted and her gaze sobered. "I'll keep it simple. It's an important spot for Dane. If you like him anywhere near as much as it looks like you do, then you need to know what matters to him."

Chloe didn't know how it was possible, but she blushed even harder, her face hot. She ignored it. "How much does it look like I like him?"

Roxanne smiled, her smile soft and warm now. "Honey, you're blushing like a schoolgirl. I may not know much, but I have some sense. Maybe it's just a crush, but you don't strike me as that type. And if Jake is telling you to ask Dane to take you to Shadow Rock, he knows Dane is in deep. Now if you ask me how that could happen so fast, I can't tell you, but there's a few areas I trust my instincts and matters of the heart are one of 'em."

Chloe felt Roxanne's words jolt through her. Crazy though she'd have thought all of this a year ago, in this moment, it felt right and true. She took a deep breath and nodded, her blush fading the tiniest bit.

"Okay then. Well, I guess I'll ask Dane to take me to Shadow Rock. Is there anything I should know before I do?"

Roxanne looked at her carefully and sighed. "Probably, but it's not for me to tell you. Do me a favor and don't forget that not everything is as it seems. We all have our heart underneath it all and that's what matters."

A prickle of awareness ran up Chloe's spine followed by a flash of annoyance that Roxanne was now being as cryptic as Jake. She lifted her chin and eyed Roxanne. "Oh, so now you too?"

Roxanne appeared to know exactly what Chloe meant. She shrugged and grinned. "Hey, I'm as straight as I can be, but this is Dane's to explain."

"Fair enough. I'll be asking him today." She shifted carefully on her feet and turned to leave. "Nice to meet you, Roxanne."

"Ditto. I hope to see you again soon," Roxanne said with a wide smile.

Chloe walked out, disconcerted by the cryptic comments by Jake and Roxanne. She worried Dane was hiding something from her—but she trusted him. But then again, she'd trusted Tom and that had turned out to be a sham.

Chapter 6

Dane strode up to Chloe's hotel door and knocked. She opened the door wide and smiled. He reined in the urge to pick her up and take them right back to where they'd been last night, tangled up in each other's arms. Her honey hair fell in tousled waves around her shoulders. Her forest green eyes were bright and...curious.

"Can you take me to Shadow Rock?" she asked, skipping past any greeting.

He instantly wondered who she'd encountered today because only close friends knew of Shadow Rock, and if they were mentioning it to her, they were dropping some pretty obvious hints. Dane swore silently. He needed to get this out of the way before they could go any further, but damn if he knew how to go about it. Jake's reminder of how disastrous it had been for him didn't help Dane figure out how to go about this.

For the moment, he'd have to play it by ear. "Could we start with hello?" he said wryly.

Chloe smiled widely. "Hello, how was your day?"

He chuckled. "It was okay. How about you?"

She nodded firmly. "Good. I walked around town…"

He couldn't stop from interrupting her. "You walked? You should have called me. You need to take it easy with your ankle."

She rolled her eyes and sighed. "I knew you'd say that. I promise I was careful. I had the ankle brace on all day. I even have witnesses."

"And who would they be?" he countered, figuring this might clue him in to who told her to ask him about Shadow Rock.

"I went into Roxanne's, met her and saw Jake again."

"Ah, Roxanne's. That place might be the center of the universe as far as Catamount is concerned." His mind spun, wondering what Roxanne and Jake had said to Chloe. He knew he needed to find a way to talk to her, but he'd have liked a little time to consider how to go about it.

Chloe grinned. "I can see that. Roxanne told me she's known you for your whole life. Jake's the one who told me to ask you about Shadow Rock."

Dane instantly felt chagrined. Here he was trying to figure out how to surreptitiously discover who said what to her while Chloe was an open book. He made a flash decision. If he wanted what he hoped for with Chloe to happen, he couldn't drag this out. She had to know who and what he was. Though the idea terrified him. This could shatter his chances with her.

"Jake knows what's important to me. Plus, it's fair to say he's trying to hold me to what I need to do."

Chloe's eyes sobered. "What do you mean?"

Not bothering with any pretense, he spoke bluntly. "I told you, I don't want a fling. I want much more than that with you. Maybe you think I'm crazy, but I don't think you do. I think you feel it too. Jake knows me well enough to know what he saw with us the other day. So…" he paused and threaded his hand through her elbow. "Let's go."

Chloe looked bemused and curious, but she didn't deny his words. She nodded and turned to get her jacket and purse. Dane stepped past her and handed them to her. As he helped her into his truck, he formed the only plan he could think of—to tell her and then show her. He could only hope she didn't run from him.

Dane nodded and took a deep breath as he started his truck. He reached over for her hand. Lifting it, he turned it and placed a kiss in the center of her palm. He kept her hand firmly in his.

"Can I ask that you try to trust me?"

Chloe's eyes clouded for a moment, a flash of pain arcing in their depths. He knew trust wouldn't come easily for her after what her ex had done. He was banking on the depth of connection between them. They may have only just met, but their hearts, souls and bodies knew one another. She took a deep breath and nodded.

Dane began driving. He tried to think of the best way to explain what he was about to show her, but there really was no easy way to get to the point. He pulled over at an unmarked entry into the forest on the far side of town. The Appalachian Trail was miles away from here, so there were far fewer chances of encountering any people. Shadow Rock was down a short path. It was the place his father had taken him when he was a boy to show him what he was. It was the same place his grandfather had taken his father and so on through the generations. Once they were out of the truck, he took her hand and carefully led her through the trees until they reached the edge of a clearing where Shadow Rock rested at the edge—a large, flat boulder. He lifted her to sit on it.

"Is this Shadow Rock?" she asked, her voice soft in the fading light.

He nodded. "When the sun's up, it casts a shadow across most of this clearing. No other reason for its name."

Her presence kept his cat close to the surface. Passion brought that side of him out, and Chloe elicited passion as no woman ever had. He took a deep breath and met her eyes. Her forest green eyes were cautious, but open. "Chloe, I'm about to tell you something that most people don't know. It might scare you and it might make you think I'm crazy. But I have to tell you because I want you more than I've wanted anyone, and I can't go forward without you knowing who I am."

Her breasts rose and fell with her breath. Her gaze was curious with a hint of caution underneath. The evening air was cooling. A mist hovered over the trees. Dane prayed she would understand, but he didn't know if she would. She didn't reply, only nodded solemnly—so he had to put it out there and trust she could handle it.

"I'm sure you've heard the rumors about mountain lions around here, right?"

"Of course. That's why it's called Catamount. I thought I saw two the other day when I was waiting for you," she replied with a gentle shrug. "They were beautiful."

"They are real. It's just that…" He paused for a breath and then pushed forward. "…mountain lions in this area are also human. They shift between forms. I'm one of them," he said simply.

Chloe gasped. Her eyes widened. "What? I don't understand."

"Our kind were run out of our territories once this part of the country was colonized. We were pushed further and further into the woods and north. We were dying because we didn't have enough space. About two hundred and fifty years ago, the first shifters were born on Mount Katahdin. Mountain lions that could shift between human and cat form survived and the rest kept dying. All that's left of our kind in the East are shifters. My family descended from the first generation of shifters."

Chloe's eyes were wide with a hint of fear, but she didn't run and she didn't look disgusted, so he forged ahead. "We live just like you do. We work, we have jobs and we carry on. But our cat side comes out sometimes and we have to shift, so we head to the forest. We don't hurt humans because we are part human. Our human minds are with us in both forms. It's a part of me, a part that will always be there. I had to tell you before anything else happened between us."

Chloe looked around the small clearing. "Is this why you brought me here? To show me?"

Dane nodded. "You have to know who I am. And you have to know that I believe we're meant to be together. Both parts of me are drawn to you so powerfully I can't ignore it. But it's only fair that you know who I am completely."

She brought her eyes back to his. Uncertainty clashed with curiosity. "Okay," she said slowly. "Do I need to worry when you are in your other form?" She paused and shook her head rapidly. "I can't believe I'm having this conversation."

"You never need to worry about me. Ever. Mountain lions who shift are fiercely protective of those they care about. We had to become that way in order to survive. Wild mountain lions are known as solitary creatures. But we couldn't survive if we stayed that way, so we evolved. We don't ever hurt humans to begin with, but those we care about…we'd give our lives to protect them."

Chloe eyed him carefully, silent for a long moment. Then a rush of questions. "So if shifters have been around for that long, how come they say eastern mountain lions are extinct? How many families are there? And how can you be with me if I'm not a shifter?" Her questions tumbled out, one after another, her voice rising along with them.

Tension coiled tightly within him. His heart pounded. He had to find a way to help her understand she had nothing to fear, but he had to be careful. He forced himself to breathe slowly though his heart beat in agony— fearful she'd reject him.

He met her eyes through the gloaming. "You can ask as many questions as you want. Do you want me to answer yet?"

She nodded jerkily.

"People think eastern mountain lions are extinct because, in their original form, they are. We've done our best to keep our presence hidden when we shift. Our ancestors were hunted almost to extinction, so once our ancestors learned to shift, hiding was key to our safety and survival. As to how many shifter families there are, there are a lot. Catamount was founded by four families, including mine. In Catamount alone, half the population, maybe more, is made up of shifters. We haven't stayed put either. Throughout most of the eastern mountain ranges, you'll find shifters everywhere. There are rumors about our kind out West, but we don't know for certain." He paused and took a breath. "For your last question, shifters are human and mountain lion—not one or the other. That's how we can mate with humans. I'm a man who happens to be able to shift into a mountain lion. Through the generations, we've seen shifters stay healthier if they mate with humans. When shifters and humans mate, some of their children may be shifters, some of them may not. There's no way to know."

Reaching the end of her questions, he paused. She sat quietly. He felt like he was walking a tightrope—one wrong move, and he could slip off and lose his chance with her. After a long silence, she nodded slowly. He stood from the small boulder and held her eyes. "Can I show you?"

His cat was rolling under his skin, straining for release. He knew he'd have to keep a tight rein on his control because Chloe's presence peaked his desire so high he could barely contain himself. The depth of his want for her pounded through his body like a drum. Its fierceness called to the cat in him. At her nod, he shed his clothes. Her eyes were steady though he sensed a shade of fear. He walked a few feet away and closed his eyes. Shifting was smooth for lions. He'd heard for other animals it could be painful. For lions, it was fluid and graceful. In a deep breath, he released his cat and felt the rush of fur caressing his skin. In seconds, he stood on all fours. He looked back toward Chloe whose mouth had fallen open. He slowly began to walk toward her. Primal desire pulsed through his veins. He kept it reined and approached her slowly.

He stopped several feet away from her. She slowly reached a hand out to touch him. Her touch was hesitant at first, but became more confident and curious. He leaned into her hand, his purr rumbling in his chest. At the sound, she smiled tentatively. After several moments of this, Dane strolled away, his tail swaying. He closed his eyes again and called his human self back. A ripple went through his body and fur became skin in a wave. He quickly tugged his clothes back on and walked to Chloe.

***

Chloe sat in the fading light, the cool air eliciting a

shiver. She watched the wild cat amble away from her. *Dane, that's Dane. How can that be Dane?* She gave a sharp shake of her head. The last few minutes had shattered any preconceptions she had about what was real and what wasn't. She thought back to the other morning when she'd been waiting for Dane to return and had seen those two mountain lions. She wondered now if it had been Dane and another shifter, perhaps his sister. She watched his body ripple and shift from cat back to human. He stood in the dusk, his human form taking her breath away. He was lean and muscular, his shoulders broad. His skin gleamed even in the faded light. She felt momentarily shy to realize he was completely nude. She tried not to stare. He strode to where his clothes had fallen and dressed quickly.

He came to stand in front of her, his eyes uncertain. He reached for her hands. The air had chilled rapidly since they arrived here, the sun's warmth dissipating as it dropped down the sky behind the mountains. His hands were warm and held hers gently. His thumb rubbed across the back of her hand.

"I hope I didn't scare you," he said, his voice low.

Chloe tried understand what she was feeling. It wasn't fear. More akin to an enormous sense of what the universe held. Watching Dane shift into cat form and back again had been so powerful, unbelievable and magical at once, it was as if any imaginary doors in her mind had been blown off their hinges. She finally looked up into his blue-gray eyes. "You didn't scare me," she said softly.

An owl hooted nearby. A rustle came from the trees. Dane held her gaze. "Do you understand why I needed to make sure you knew who I was?"

Chloe nodded solemnly.

"Does it change anything for you?"

This time she shook her head. The girl she'd been

for so long, the one who planned and did what she thought she was supposed to, would have had no idea what to think about who and what Dane was. The woman she'd become after reality landed with a thud in her life and she'd hiked over two thousand miles in commune with nature every step of the way—that woman had come to learn there was so much humans didn't know. Nature in all its forms held so much magic. Learning Dane was a man who was also a mountain lion, while mind-blowing, didn't change what she felt when she was near him. She shook her head. A sharp breeze gusted over her skin, and she shivered.

Dane pushed to standing again and gave her a soft tug. "Let's go. You're getting cold."

They walked hand and hand to his truck and drove through the falling dark to his house. Chloe barely noticed the details of his home when they arrived. She had a brief impression of warm wood. Her heart beat like soft wings in her chest.

Chapter 7

Dane paused to kick his shoes off when he entered the house, Chloe's hand in his. He flicked the lights on and immediately lifted her in his arms, walking through the entryway and up the stairs that curved along the wall of the entry. Ever since he'd shifted in front of her, and she hadn't freaked out, all he could think about was finally being with her the way he wanted. Thinking wasn't quite the word to describe what was happening. More that he was driven by pure instinct. It had taken every ounce of restraint he owned inside to stop when he did last night with her. The thin thread he clung to had been thrown by his conscience —he couldn't let himself go further at the time, knowing what she didn't know and how that held the potential to ruin any chance with her. But tonight, she knew who and what he was. While he sensed all was not settled just yet, he wasn't going to wait any longer unless she insisted.

And Chloe showed no sign of that. On the ride home, her hand had stayed warm in his. Just now, her breath caught when he lifted her. With her held close against his chest, he glanced down, his eyes colliding with hers. The air fairly crackled around them. He sucked his breath in sharply. He forced himself to keep moving, taking long strides down the hall once he cleared the top stair. Her heart thudded against his chest, his own pulse surging in reply. He turned the corner into his bedroom. In three strides, he reached his bed, a massive mahogany canopy bed passed down through the generations of his family.

He carefully set Chloe down before flicking on a single lamp by the bed. When he turned, he found her looking curiously around the room. His bedroom was an expansive room. He'd inherited his parents' home, which had been in his family since the day it was built in the early eighteen hundreds. It was a colonial style farmhouse, average by the standards of its time, but rambling in the modern era. His bedroom had enough space for his bed, a lounging area with couches and books, and a dressing room to the side with a massive master bathroom. Aside from the bed, he'd updated the entire room with modern, comfortable furniture.

One look at Chloe with her hair catching sparks in the lamplight, her green eyes gleaming, her skin honeyed as her hair was, and Dane had to close his eyes and breathe to keep from allowing his cat instincts to gain control and take her too aggressively. That time would come, but not tonight. A few deep breaths, and he opened his eyes. Stepping in front of her, he knelt and removed the air brace and the practical running shoe on her other foot, careful not to disturb her sprained ankle. He stroked his palms up her thighs. Her breath hitched, and his cock throbbed in response.

He tilted his head up and met her eyes. "Is this okay?" His words rasped in the quiet room.

Her pulse was visible in her neck as she nodded. "More than okay."

Protected Mate (Catamount Lion Shifters)

He moved swiftly, standing and tearing his clothes off. He didn't intend to rush once they were skin to skin, but he couldn't bear to delay that. She held his eyes steadily as he stood in front of her, his arousal blatant. He leaned forward, his hands on either side of her hips, and paused with his lips a whisper away. He meant to say something, but before he could she slipped her hand around his neck and tugged his mouth to hers. Chloe's combination of shy and bold was intoxicating.

Her tongue stroked across his lips, her mouth fell open, and their kiss exploded. Dane could barely keep his balance and shifted to kneel between her knees. He cupped her face in his hands, delving deeply into her mouth. Her hands traveled down his chest, her soft touch sending sparks skittering in its wake. He trailed his lips down her neck, pausing when he reached the collar of her shirt, a soft t-shirt that hugged her ample breasts. He slipped a hand underneath, dragging her shirt up. In a swift move, she leaned back and tugged it over her head. Before he could catch his breath, she unsnapped her bra and tossed it aside.

The sight of her bare breasts took his breath away. His heart raced with want, lust surged through his body. In a flash, she pushed him back and stood. He reflexively grabbed her hips to steady her.

"Easy with your ankle," he said, his voice husked with desire.

Her lips curved in a soft smile. "I know you've got me. I just want my jeans off. I'm guessing you might like that too."

Her mischievous smile only turned the heat up a notch for him. He lifted his hands away for her to slide her jeans over her hips and shimmy out of them. And then she stood before him in a pair of bright red cotton panties. Her breasts were inches away, and he didn't hesitate to lean

57

forward and lave one nipple and then the other, rolling her nipples between his thumb a forefinger, savoring the heavy weight of her breasts in his palms. With a firm stroke of his palm gliding down her abdomen, he pushed her back. She lay back with a sigh, a soft moan escaping when he slid a hand down to cup her mound, the moist heat of her desire pulsing through the cotton.

He had to fight to keep from tearing her panties off and plunging inside of her. His cock was so hard it bordered on painful. But more than that…he wanted to imprint this experience on her and savored the anticipation of knowing how much better it would be if he didn't rush. He circled his thumb against her clit through the cotton. Her hips shifted restlessly with her gasp. He trailed slow kisses up the inside of her thigh and slipped a finger under the edge of her panties. Her folds were drenched with desire. His intentions weakened when she gasped.

"Dane…"

"Hmm?"

"Don't make me wait…"

He smiled against her skin and hooked a finger on the edge of her panties, swiftly dragging them down.

"Just a minute…"

The cat in him flexed and arched, the primal drive to plunge into her so intense, he had to clench his teeth. He finally brought his mouth against her, her hips bucking into him the moment he slid his tongue up and down her folds and coasted across the nub of her desire. The salty tang of her was like a drug. He laid a palm on the soft curve of her belly using his other hand to tease in her folds and give in to the long, slow taste of her.

Chloe went wild against his mouth and hand, her cries echoing through him. Time dissolved as he lost himself watching her fly apart. When her channel clenched

and she cried his name, his snatched a condom out of his
jeans on the floor and rolled it on, stretching full length
over her body as she shuddered. In a swift move, he tugged
both hands above her head, holding them in place with one
hand, finally giving in to his need to dominate. He paused
and said her name. Her mossy green eyes blinked open. He
cupped her cheek with his free hand and held her gaze. Her
bare body felt so good against his, he was stunned. She
licked her lips and shifted under him.

"Now…" she said.

He surged inside of her, her wet channel hugging
him tightly. Her eyes widened, her breath came in ragged
gasps. She shifted her hips, opening her thighs wider and
arching against him. His last hold on control broke and he
pulled back to thrust deeper inside of her. He lost himself in
the rhythm. He held her pinned against the bed as he gave
in and allowed the tempest inside of him to take over,
surging and stroking into her, deeper and deeper each time.
She suddenly gasped his name and he felt her climax ripple
around him. His own crashed over him in a wave.

***

Dane growled her name and arched back, plunging
deeply into her. Chloe was awash in the orgasm that had
blown her apart. The feel of him inside was beyond
anything she could have imagined. By the time he finally
entered her, the ache to have him inside was so intense, she
was near out of her mind. The fullness filled an empty
place in her body and her soul that she hadn't known she
had. He collapsed against her, his hand easing its grip on
her wrists. He shifted his weight to the side and lay still.
His breath gusted against her shoulder. He trailed a hand
down her cheek, lightly tracing her collarbone, curling
softly around her breast and coming to rest on the curve of

her abdomen.

She lay still, trying to catch her breath and to think. The entirety of her sexual life, she'd assumed she simply couldn't relax enough to have an orgasm. Dane's mere presence with her had made it happen with such ease, she couldn't have stopped it if she tried. The feeling was so utterly delicious. Her mind rolled back to earlier tonight when he'd all but blown her mind. She still couldn't quite wrap her brain around what he was even though she'd seen it with her own eyes. And though a part of her wasn't so sure what to think, if she listened to her heart, her body and her soul rather than her oh-so-controlling mind, she trusted him more completely than she'd ever trusted anyone.

She rolled her head to the side to find his blue-gray eyes on hers in the soft glow of light from the single lamp. Holding her gaze, he leaned forward and gave her a lingering kiss before rolling away. He stood and walked across his huge bedroom to a door she presumed led to the bathroom. She heard water running, and then he returned, striding toward her. The sight of him took her breath away. He was all lean, sinewy muscle, his skin burnished gold. When he reached the side of the bed, he slid an arm under her hips and lifted her easily.

"Where are we going?" she asked as he started to carry her across the room.

"Shower."

Though she loved being held in his arms, she protested. "I can walk…"

His intense blue-gray eyes slanted down to hers. "You're ankle still isn't up to speed. Plus…" He paused with a sly grin. "It gives me another reason to touch you."

His words sent a shiver through her and warmth curling around her heart. Dane stepped through the doorway into a large dressing room with closets lining the walls. In another few steps, they entered the master bathroom, another huge room. Chloe's impression of the home had been so brief when they'd entered, it was only now sinking in that this was an old farmhouse with gleaming hardwood floors in most rooms and elaborate tile in the bathroom. As with many older homes, the rooms were much larger than those of modern homes. The bathroom had clearly been updated with a soaking tub occupying one corner and a shower tiled in soothing blue glass. He set her down just outside the shower. Steam billowed out when he opened the glass door and gestured for her to enter. He kept a hand firmly on her elbow as she stepped inside.

She was still readjusting to the sheer heaven of hot water after so many months of hiking and quick baths in cold rivers, streams and lakes along the way. She sighed at the feel of water coasting over her skin. Mist curled around them. Dane moved with efficiency as he quickly soaped himself and then turned to her. Though his movements were quick, every touch was a caress. Chloe didn't realize how tired she was until he lifted her again and carried her back to his bed. Cool sheets fell against her skin, followed by a down quilt and then the heat of Dane's body curling around her.

Chapter 8

A few days later, Dane bumped the swinging door that led to the break room with his shoulder. He'd had a busy morning at his family practice between ear infections, a broken arm, and a little boy whose curiosity got the best of him when he encountered a porcupine in the woods. The porcupine, a creature rather inclined to avoid confrontation, had scurried away, but the little boy followed it. For his trouble, the boy only came away with a few quills in his arm, but he was wailing loudly enough, he terrified his mother. Dane filled a cup of coffee and headed straight for his office. After flying through paperwork to get charts up to date in the electronic records system, his phone buzzed. Seeing Chloe's number, he answered immediately.

"Hey there," he said.

"So what time did you say we were meeting for dinner at The Trailhead?"

Dane glanced at his watch, smiling because he couldn't help but smile whenever he heard Chloe's voice. "Six."

"Okay. I'll meet you there."

"I'll pick you up," he countered. "Your ankle's almost better, but you're not helping with your insistence on walking as much as you have."

Her ankle sprain was almost healed, but not because of her efforts. He'd quickly discovered when left to her own devices, Chloe ignored most of his recommendations, namely that she liked walking around town. Though he didn't want to argue the point because she'd also finally agreed to stay at his house instead of at the inn. When they were together, Dane knew beyond any doubt, she was meant to be with him. But when they weren't skin to skin, he could see the wheels turning in her brain. Though she claimed she hadn't had a plan when she finished hiking the trail, he was fairly certain she'd never contemplated meeting a mountain lion shifter who insisted they were meant to be together.

"Dane, you have to stop insisting on driving me everywhere. How about I rent a car?"

"I'll find one for you to borrow. How's that?"

Chloe laughed. "Fine. I suppose there's no point in debating whether it's okay for me to walk to meet you for dinner," she said cheekily.

"I know you're tired of taking it easy with your ankle, but I don't want you to aggravate the sprain. If you don't mind me picking you up..."

"I don't mind, but after that, I'm renting a car tomorrow, or we find one for me to borrow."

Dane hung up a few moments later and wondered how soon was too soon to ask Chloe to consider something more permanent with him. The last few days had been a bubble of shimmering passion, which only served to ratchet up his need for her. He was trying to balance the need to give her space with his own need to find a way to know if she felt what he felt. The mere thought that she'd stay for a visit and then leave Catamount made his heart clench. He wished like hell he wasn't trying to deal with the fallout from Callen's death in the midst of this. It chafed on his conscience that he couldn't talk much about his concerns about what happened to Callen. He worried she picked up that he was holding something back and misunderstood what it might mean.

His phone buzzed again. This time Jake's number flashed on the screen. "What's up?" he answered brusquely.

"You got a minute?" Jake asked.

"Just finishing up at work. Do you want me to stop by?"

"That'd be good. I'll be in my office for another half hour. Can you make it before then?"

Dane clicked off his computer and stood. "On my way."

Minutes later, he rested a hip against Jake's desk. Jake's office was a few blocks away from his. Jake had multiple computer screens covering his desk. The hum from his computer server was constant. Jake claimed he needed a separate office from home, or he'd never take a break. Dane had seen the lights on at his office at all hours, so he could imagine it would be much worse if Jake didn't keep some type of divide between home and work.

"So?" Dane asked.

Jake swung around in his chair, his eyes serious. "You're not going to like this," he said flatly.

Dane gut coiled. "Just tell me Callen didn't risk our safety by accidentally revealing who we are to the government."

"I can't say he did that, but I can't say he didn't. I don't even know what to do with what I found. I'll say this much: this needs to stay between you and me until we get a better idea of what was going on."

The knot of worry in Dane's gut tightened. If Jake thought they needed to keep this quiet, it could only be bad news. He eyed Jake carefully. "You know I won't say anything. What the hell did you find?"

Jake took a deep breath and leaned his elbows on the desk. "So I hacked into the email of the Fish and Wildlife guy, Hayden Thorne, and did a lot more digging into Callen's computer files. Far as I can tell, he's nothing more than a red herring. I think he might be able to help us, but I don't think he's our problem. Callen was working with some guy out in Montana to sell..." Jake paused and shook his head. "Damn if I know how to describe it, but here goes. I think Callen was trying to sell our services for some high end money."

"What the hell does that mean?"

Jake ran a hand through his hair. His eyes were bloodshot, his clothes rumpled, and his hair looked as if he'd run a hand through it too many times to count. "Callen had multiple email accounts under different aliases. The surface one, the one we first looked at, was the only one he used to communicate with Hayden. He seemed to be trying to pump him for information. I wouldn't be surprised to find out that Hayden's a shifter himself. But that's another issue altogether. Anyway, he used some other accounts to communicate with a guy—no idea who this guy is, never mentions any names—and the deal was Callen offered this guy shifters to use for drug smuggling. For some serious money."

Dane's stomach felt like lead. "You can't be serious. There's got to be a mistake."

Jake shook his head slowly. "Trust me, I said the same thing to myself. I've been up almost day and night combing through these email accounts. Once I tracked down the alias accounts, I almost lost it. I didn't want to say anything until I knew for sure I could trace everything back to Callen. He did a decent job of covering his tracks, but he wasn't savvy enough to know how to mask his internet service provider address completely, so that's how I linked everything back to him. I can show you all of it. I've saved it on a separate flash drive and backed it up to in the cloud and on two separate hard drives to be on the safe side."

Dane tried to absorb what Jake was saying, but he was stunned. He and Callen hadn't been particularly close, but he'd trusted him. To think Callen was slinking around, trying to find ways to make money off of their shifter clan, blew his mind. And broke his heart. If Shana found out about this, she'd be devastated on a new level. It would shake the foundation of the love she had for Callen. Then there was the issue of how much risk Callen brought down on them. The existence of shifters was protected knowledge. That's how they survived. For Callen to expose them to the seedy and dangerous world of drug smuggling, well, it was damning and terrifying.

Dane looked up and met Jake's eyes, deep blue and dead serious. "You're pretty confident about this then?"

Jake nodded slowly. "As confident as I can be without catching him red-handed in the middle of sending these emails. The digital fingerprints are damning. The only other consideration would be someone else at the same ISP address. But I already did my homework on that. It meant I had to rule Shana out, so I crosschecked her work schedule against the times the emails were sent. Every single email was sent during one of her work shifts. If there's one good thing about working at the hospital, it's that they keep employee logs online. Everything is tracked, even when people call out sick. She was verified on duty whenever Callen was busy online. I even checked client records to confirm she was seeing patients during those times. Much as it turns my stomach with Callen, I can see it. He was always looking for ways to capitalize on shifter powers. Remember that bullshit he used to spew about it in high school? He toned it down after we got through college, but I'm thinking it's more that he realized if he didn't shut up about it, we might look a little too hard."

Dane shook his head sharply. "Damn. I just…don't know what the hell to think. I'd have been pissed if you told me you had to rule Shana out, but I'm glad you did. This way, we don't even have to ask her about it."

Dane paused and stared across the desk at Jake. Jake's eyes stared steadily back, bleary, sad and angry.

"This sucks," Dane said quietly.

"Tell me about it. We've got a town full of people mourning Callen's death when they have no idea what he was doing behind our backs."

"So any idea where Callen went? Did he actually go to Montana? Or was that a cover too?"

"Oh, he was there. The digital trail goes dark as far as who he met with and what he did. All I have are locations of where he was meeting people, but that doesn't help much. I know he was supposed to deliver a 'package' to someone. He offered to demonstrate the utility of our travel capabilities. I mean, who the hell would think a mountain lion was smuggling drugs? The route was supposed to be across the border into Canada. It's obvious something went wrong because he got tagged and headed east only to get hit by a car in Connecticut. Though for all we know, he was supposed to be in Connecticut. There's definitely a market for drugs there, but it's damn busy for travel. Not to mention that mountain lions haven't been seen in the East for almost a century if you're not counting the myths about us. If he hadn't been hit by a car, the presence of a mountain lion anywhere near Connecticut would have drawn tons of attention, which is exactly what happened."

Dane was still struggling to wrap his brain around what Jake told him, but enough of it was sinking in to permeate into a cold fury inside. He met Jake's tired gaze. "Back to your earlier point, I forgot how much Callen used to make noise about how we didn't even know how to use the powers we had. I chalked it up to him being young and arrogant. His dad was on the obnoxious side too, so I didn't think much of it." He paused and sighed. "What the hell are we going to do now?"

Jake shook his head slowly. "Damn if I know. For the moment, let me keep digging and see what else I find. We need to keep this quiet. I'd like to reach out to Hayden Thorne. He seemed to be on the up and up. I got the sense he was concerned about Callen's questions. For all we know, he's aware of whoever these people were that wanted to use shifters for their smuggling operations. In the meantime, we can't say a word, not even to Shana."

Dane nodded. "You'll get no argument from me there. Do we know if Callen revealed our location to anyone?"

"Not that I found so far. But all it would take was someone like me on the other side to chase down his digital trail. We can't sit on this for too long."

Dane stood. "I know. Let me know what I can do. Let's talk again tomorrow. In the meantime, I told Chloe I'd meet her for dinner, so I gotta get going."

Jake's eyes sharpened. "Have you told her anything yet?"

"Oh right. I haven't seen you the last few days. Thanks to you telling her to ask me about Shadow Rock, I had to think on my feet, but she handled it. I should seriously thank you. I probably would have kept putting it off because I was afraid she'd run. She still has a lot of questions, but I think it'll be okay. Now I just have to convince her to stay in Catamount."

Jake's eyes widened. "You're really serious about her?"

Dane nodded firmly. "I told you the first time I saw her, I knew she was the one for me. I'm not playing games here. I wish like hell this mess around Callen wasn't happening because I think she knows something's up. I'm trying to figure out how to explain without getting into all the details. And now with this new information, we have a lot more to worry about."

Jake nodded slowly. "That's putting it lightly. I'll call you tomorrow," he said, swinging his chair back around and immediately clicking onto his computer again.

***

"Who are you talking about?" Dane asked Chloe.

They were at dinner at The Trailhead, and Chloe was telling him about a man she met at Roxanne's today. Dane felt his hackles rise for what appeared to be no reason. All he knew was his gut pinged loudly when Chloe mentioned the man.

She'd just taken a bite of food and held a finger up while she chewed. After a quick sip of water, she glanced up, her mossy green eyes temporarily distracting him. He could look at her all day every day and never tire of it. She was so damn beautiful and completely unaware of how sensual she was. She tucked a lock of hair behind her ear. "I thought he was someone else from Catamount. He said his name was Seth. Honestly, I assumed he was a shifter. Now that I know they're real, I've been paying attention. Like how you, Shana and Jake all have eyes that tip up at the corners. And you move like a cat."

Dane choked on his water. "I don't move like a cat when I'm not in lion form."

Chloe wrinkled her nose and shook her head. "Yes you do. Anyway, back to this guy. He was asking me how I met you and stuff. I figured he knew you. It's not crazy I'd think that. Half this damn town asks me nosy questions about you. They're all protective and stuff. As if I'm somehow a risk to you," she said huffily. "When seriously, I'm not the one that can shift into a mountain lion. I'm just a plain old person with a bum ankle."

Dane grinned at her comment. Catamount wasn't too small, not anymore, but locals were protective. He knew those close to him weren't worried about Chloe the way she meant. They were worried the way all shifters worried about humans finding out about their existence. He didn't expect the dust to settle on that until he and Chloe were a sure thing. Until then, there would be fears she'd reveal them to outsiders. His mind turned to this man Chloe mentioned. He didn't know anyone named Seth. It made him seriously uncomfortable to know this guy clearly knew who he was. On the heels of what Jake had discovered about Callen's dealings, Dane's instincts were on high alert.

Chloe tilted her head, her eyes assessing. "Why do you look so worried?"

He looked across the table at her—her open eyes, her warmth, everything about her was straightforward. Her default was to trust others. He loved that about her. The only place where she seemed leery was when it came to love. He needed to cue her in however he could. Not just to keep her safe, but he didn't like hiding anything from her. He was determined to show her she could trust him.

"Because just like there's good people and bad people, there are good shifters and bad shifters. I don't know anyone named Seth, so whoever this guy is he was trying to make it seem like he knew me when he doesn't. That's usually not a good thing." He paused and took a breath, watching her carefully. Her eyes were serious, but not frightened.

She circled her fingertip around the top of her wineglass. "Is this about whatever it is that's got you so worried?"

"How do you know I'm worried?"

Chloe's shoulder rose and fell in a tiny shrug. "I know we haven't known each long…" When she paused, her cheeks were pink. "But I feel like I've known you a lot longer. You're not telling me something. If you want me to give us a chance, like you say, it's not going to help if you hide things from me."

Dane looked at her carefully. "I don't want to hide anything from you, so please don't think it's that. I'll try to explain as much as I can. I'm sure you've heard how people are pretty upset about Callen's death." At Chloe's nod, he continued. "I don't even think I had a chance to explain he was a shifter. It's true he died in a car accident, but he was the mountain lion that got killed on the highway in Connecticut."

Chloe's hand flew to her mouth. "Oh my God. That's awful! What happened? Why was he there?" Her questions tumbled out, the same questions so many others had asked.

Dane's stomach felt like lead to consider Callen's death in the context of what he knew now. "I don't know why he was there. None of us do. So that's got me and plenty of other people freaked out. Jake's been helping me look into some of Callen's computer files. I can't go into the details now, but I'll tell you that I'm far more worried than I was to begin with about how and why Callen died

71

and what it might mean for us here. We're not the only mountain lion shifters in the country. There are others. Callen was trying to find them and make contact. We're worried he may have made the wrong connections. That's why this Seth guy approaching you and acting like he knows me has me worried. I wish I could tell you more, but honestly I don't know much more."

Chloe swirled her finger around the wineglass again, her expression pensive. "Wow. I didn't know that's why everyone was so upset about Callen. I figured he meant a lot to people and they were grieving. Knowing there's something else behind it is scary. Does everyone know about this?"

Dane shook his head. "Everyone knows he was looking to make contact with other shifters and is pretty scared about how he died and how he got tagged. Jake and I are working on this and need some more time. I haven't even given you all the details because I can't yet. I wanted to tell you what I could. I don't want to put you in danger."

Chloe nodded slowly. "I understand. Thank you for telling me what you could. You don't have to give me all the details, but it helps a lot to have some idea. Otherwise…well, my mind had all kinds of ideas and most of them have nothing to do with that." She shrugged again, pain flashing through her eyes. "You're nothing like Tom, but what he did makes me question that anyone would want me. When I'm with you, I don't think about things like that. But when I'm not, my mind can go all kinds of places."

"Chloe, I understand why you might think that because of what Tom did, but he was an idiot. You're absolutely amazing. All I want is you. I'm only holding back so I don't scare you," Dane said flatly.

Chapter 9

Chloe walked into Dane's house ahead of him, his hand warm on her low back. She thought about what he'd said at dinner and wondered if she had the courage to take the leap he was asking of her. She'd felt it the first time she saw him in the shadowy cave—a magnetic pull. Behind it lay the sense that she couldn't shake—she was meant to find him. If she kept her head quiet, her heart knew she'd likely never feel what she felt with anyone else. She'd believed she loved Tom, but when she considered her feelings for him in context now, they were but a shadow, a thin imitation of what she felt for Dane. It was a connection on a level beyond intellect. It was the depth of their connection that cushioned her fear when he explained who he was and showed her.

Dane closed the door behind them, the sound echoing against the tiled entryway. She glanced up and around the room. The home had a formal entrance with stairs winding up along a curved wall that led to the landing on the upper floor. He'd explained he'd inherited the home from his parents after they both passed away. The home had been built by his great-grandparents and was a sprawling, elegant colonial home. It had been updated with modern appliances and was furnished with a mix of antique heirlooms and modern furniture. Chloe sensed Dane loved the home for the comfort it offered, but it felt lonely, as if it needed much more than his presence to fill it.

She'd called her mother the other day to check in, letting her know her ankle was mostly healed, and she was considering staying in Catamount. She hadn't told Dane how seriously she was considering it. She turned the pebbles of her thoughts in her mind. Her mother had been nothing but supportive, as she always was. She'd been puzzled when Chloe abruptly quit her job and began planning for her hike, but her mother had surprised her with her openness. She seemed relieved to know Chloe was in one place before winter set in.

Chloe turned to find Dane watching her quietly. The entrance was shadowed with only one light on by the stairs. His blue-gray eyes met hers, her heart leaping in response to the bare *want* she saw in their depths. After so much doubt about herself after what happened with Tom, she felt desired and desirable when she was with Dane. Doubt never crossed her mind when they were together. What lay between them felt so right, so true and so powerful, her mind didn't have a chance to convince her otherwise. She tugged his hand into hers and turned to the stairs.

"Come on," she said softly.

He followed without a word until she stepped onto the landing and felt his hands curl around her hips and slide down to cup her bottom. Just like that, and she was wet. She was almost always toeing the edge of full-blown desire when she was near him, but when he touched her, she was gone. A throaty sound came from him. She'd gone shopping yesterday and wore a skirt she'd bought. After so many months of dressing in nothing beyond what was practical, she couldn't resist wearing it tonight though it wasn't practical. It was bordering on too cold, but she'd worn the green gauzy skirt that twirled around her knees anyway. Though Dane would dispute this, she did make an effort to be careful with her ankle and had worn the skirt with a pair of low heels though they weren't as feminine as she'd have liked.

She gasped when she felt his heated hands slide up her calves and under her skirt. With no hesitation, he hooked a finger on the edge of her panties and slipped them down. He steadied her and helped her step out of her shoes. With a flick of his wrist, her panties slid across the hardwood floor. Her efforts at wowing him with the lacy thong she'd purchased were wasted. She began to turn and he held her still.

"Wait," he said, his voice low and taut.

He stepped up to the landing and turned her to face the railing. Her hands curled around it, the wood cool in her grasp. His hands cupped her bottom again, this time through her skirt, which had fallen again. The heat of his palms stoked the fire inside of her. Delicious anticipation curled through her. In a swift move, one of his hands came around and tore at her blouse, the buttons coming undone, some flying off, echoing in the hall as they hit the floor. Another flick of his hand and her bra fell to the floor. His other hand tugged her skirt down until it pooled around her ankles. She was bare now, her skin pebbling in the cool air, a relief against the flushed heat of desire racing through her.

The denim of his jeans brushed against her when he pressed his hips into her. She could feel the heat of his cock and couldn't stop her hips from pushing back into the cradle of his. He groaned before moving away and sliding a hand down around her bottom and into her folds, drenched with the evidence of her desire. Her back arched as she pushed into his hand, his fingers stroking in and out of her.

His other hand toyed with her nipples, while his lips landed on her low back and moved up her spine in a meticulous and devastating path. She couldn't have known that slow kisses marching up her spine would bring her to the edge of desperation. His fingers moved in and out of her at the same pace, his thumb cresting across her clit again and again. When he reached her neck and softly bit her, she tumbled over the edge, shattering with a scream that echoed in the entryway.

His head fell into the dip between her shoulder and neck, his breath gusting against her skin. They stayed like for long moments. The heat of his arousal pressed against her hips. Her senses were scrambled, but her mind finally pulled itself together enough for her to lift her head. With a small turn of her face, her lips met his. Before she could speak, he lifted her into his arms and carried her down the dark hallway into his bedroom. A room she'd come to think of as *theirs*. Her mind shied away from that thought.

Dane flicked a light on and carried her to the bed. When he set her down, she took matters into her own hands and immediately tugged him to her. She cupped his heated length through the rough denim on his jeans and glanced up at him. He closed his eyes with a deep breath and began to step back.

"No," she said firmly, moving quickly to tear his jeans open and free his cock. Without giving him more time to take control, she leaned forward and took him in her mouth. He groaned deeply and gasped her name.

With a soft hum, she took him all the way into her mouth, the head of his shaft bumping the back of her throat. She tugged his jeans down, hooking her toes over the waistband once she got them past his hips and dragging them to the floor. He again tried to shift back. She'd come to learn he liked to take charge when they made love. He did it so masterfully, she not only didn't mind—she luxuriated in it. But now, for just a little while, she wanted to have him at her mercy.

She cupped his balls in her hand, rolling them softly. She pulled back slowly, maintaining wet suction as she did, and commenced to stroke her tongue up and down his shaft. She wrapped a hand around him and began to slowly glide up and down. Dane's breathing was ragged, his head thrown back.

"Chloe…" he choked out. "Just…let me…"

She giggled when his words trailed off as she curled her tongue around the head and took him back in her mouth in one deep glide to the base. She swiftly pulled away and paused, dragging her thumb in a slow stroke up. A drop of cum glistened, and she brought her lips in soft kiss to take it in.

Suddenly, he moved swiftly. She was lifted up and back, landing in the pile of pillows on his bed. He turned her so she faced away and propped a pillow under her hips. In seconds, she was on fire and desperate for him to fill her. He toyed with her nipples, one hand coming underneath and tugging softly on them. His other hand trailed in lazy circles on her bottom, barely coasting past where her wet center ached for him. In increments, he teased her thighs apart until she was spread wide for him. He was devastatingly gentle and rough at once—so arousing, she was consumed with want.

Just when she didn't think she could bear it, he shifted behind her. She heard the distinct sound of a condom wrapper and felt his heated shaft against her cleft before he surged inside. He thrust to the hilt, seating himself deeply. She almost came instantly, but he became still for a long moment. And then…slow, long, hot, and deep strokes. She lost herself in a haze of arousal and aching pleasure. Each stroke was flint against her desperation until she quivered and exploded in release. He plunged deeply once more, a guttural cry burst out as he convulsed inside of her. He remained behind her, their breath echoing in the quiet room.

He finally withdrew slowly, standing to dispose of the condom in the bathroom and returning. She was so limp from her release, she remained collapsed on the pillows. When the bed shifted under his weight, she turned her head to find his blue-gray eyes on her.

"I suppose I should move," she said softly.

"You're getting cold," he replied, running his hand down her arm, making her aware her skin was pebbled from the chilled air.

Chloe had been rendered almost incoherent and hadn't even registered she was cold. With a sigh, she rolled over. Dane tugged the comforter out from under them while she rearranged the pillows. She collapsed against his chest once he tucked the fluffy down quilt over them. His body was a furnace, always emanating heat. She tangled her legs in his and snuggled close. His warm palm moved in lazy strokes up and down her back. In moments, she was warmed through.

He spoke softly. "Chloe…"

She glanced up from where her head rested on his shoulder. His eyes were serious eliciting a flicker of concern inside of her. While diving into the depth of passion between them and following her heart's lead to trust him, her mind had its moments of concern.

At her glance, he cleared his throat. "I don't know how much longer I can do this if I don't know what you're thinking about us." His words were weighted. She sensed he was torn.

She looked at him. The lamplight cast across his skin, which always looked as if was glowing from within— a warm, golden tone. His dark gold hair fell in a rumple across his forehead. His eyes, oh those eyes. She could look at them all day and night and never tire of it. Intent, focused and so compelling it took her breath away. If anyone would have told her she'd meet a man and she would know, almost instantly, that they were meant to be together, she'd have laughed. Under that laugh would have run the vein of bitterness laid in the grooves of her heart from coming face to face with what trying to do the right thing had shown her.

On the surface, Dane was everything she would have once thought ridiculous. He was a sexually charged man who emanated that charge wherever he went. His confidence was complete. Not even taking into consideration that he was a mountain lion shifter, she'd have steered far clear of him in the days when her tidy, planning brain ran her life. But now, her heart told her what her mind would have thought to question. He was the most logical choice ever because no one else would be, or could be, what he was to her, what they were together.

She met his blue-gray eyes in the soft light. "I'm staying in Catamount," she said simply. "I'd like to stay with you if that's okay."

Dane's eyes held hers, the connection between them arcing. His gaze was fierce, so focused it startled her.

"Is that okay?" she asked, suddenly not sure.

Dane nodded sharply, tugging her hand into his and placing it over his heart, which pounded fiercely under her palm. "It's more than okay. It's everything I wanted, but I didn't want to push too fast." His voice was gruff, his eyes pinned to hers. His features softened slowly, and he tipped his head forward, and he took her lips in a slow kiss before tugging her head into his chest and wrapping his arms around her tightly. His heart pounded against hers. She fell asleep to the soft drum of his heartbeat.

Chapter 10

A few days later, Dane shouldered through the door at Roxanne's first thing in the morning and headed to the coffee counter. The tables there were filled with locals, but one man was definitely not local. Dane wondered if he was the Seth who'd approached Chloe asking about him. He had light brown hair and gray eyes. Dane knew at a glance that the man was a shifter. He lounged at a table, his manner feigning nonchalance while his energy was coiled tight. Dane walked to the counter and leaned on his elbows.

Roxanne had her back to the counter, busy at the espresso machine. When she turned around and saw him, she smiled widely. "Dane! I haven't seen you in days. You're supposed to stop by at least every other day. You know that right?"

Dane grinned in return. "I know. Been so busy, I forgot. I missed your coffee though, so I figured I'd better get myself some before you barred me for lack of attendance."

Roxanne shook her head and chuckled. "Be right back," she said, sticking a pen behind her ear and carrying a cup of coffee over to the man Dane had noticed. He watched the interaction out of the corner of his eye. Roxanne appeared guarded though polite. Her usual warmth was missing with the man.

When she returned to the counter, Dane waited quietly while she prepped his coffee—a shot in the dark, his favorite dark roast with a shot of espresso. Once she handed it over, he met her eyes and spoke quietly.

"Who's the man over there?" he asked.

Roxanne kept her voice low and her expression neutral. "Says his name is Seth. And maybe it is. But I don't trust him. He's been around town for a few days now and keeps acting like he knows people with name-dropping. In fact, he mentioned your name a few times. Says he came for Callen's funeral."

Dane gut was uneasy. "I've never seen him. Chloe mentioned that he approached her here and acted like he knew me. Any word from anyone else about him?"

Roxanne shook her head. "What's going on Dane? You and Jake are so closed-mouthed, but I know something's up. Everyone's on edge after Callen died. If you know something, would you mind filling me in?"

Dane wished like hell he could tell Roxanne what Jake had discovered, but it would blow the emotions on this town through the sky. Callen's betrayal was so deep, it hurt Dane to think about it. He met Roxanne's warm blue eyes. "As soon as I can talk, I will. I promise."

Roxanne nodded. "Okay, could you maybe clue me in if I need to keep my eye out for anything? Being here, I either see or hear about almost everything that goes on in Catamount."

"I know you do. Do me a favor and keep an eye out if you see Chloe. I asked her to be careful, but I'm worried about Seth and what the hell he wants. Not only did he know my name, but he acted like he knew Chloe and I were together. He shouldn't know any of that."

Roxanne eyed him carefully. "Dane, half the town is chattering about you and Chloe. It's not exactly news."

"Yeah, but he's not from around here. Who would be talking to him and why would it matter to him?"

"Okay, now you got me more nervous than I already was. When is Callen's funeral?"

"Tomorrow."

Roxanne looked out over the room, bringing her eyes back to Dane. She cleared her throat. "Perhaps a change of subject is in order," she said, a grin crossing her face. "What *is* going on with you and Chloe?"

Dane chuckled. He'd wondered how long Roxanne could hold out. He'd known her his entire life and considered her a dear friend. She wasn't too interfering. Though she could be protective about her friends if she was concerned. He met her eyes and smiled. "Chloe's staying in Catamount. With me."

Roxanne's face bloomed in a huge smile. "Oh, that is the best news I've had all day!"

Dane glanced at the clock on the wall behind her. "It's only seven in the morning."

She shook her head and clapped a hand over her heart. "As soon as I saw Chloe, I knew she was for you. I'm so glad she figured it out too. I won't get into it now, but I'm assuming she knows everything she needs to know."

Dane nodded. "Yup. All's clear on that front. I think it was, uh, illuminating for her, but she seems okay with it." He hadn't quite allowed himself to feel the depth of his fear that she might reject him. Until Chloe, he'd never had to wonder if someone might reject him, or reject who and what he was, because no woman had mattered enough.

With Chloe, to even consider that she might have run from him and refused to accept him for what he was—it had terrified him. His relief at her knowing he was a shifter, seeing it with her own eyes, and still turning to him afterwards was immense. Just thinking about it sent a wash of relief through his body.

"Dane?"

He swung his eyes back to Roxanne's. "Yeah?"

Roxanne chuckled. "You were off in la-la land there for a minute. Chloe's gotten under your skin, huh?"

Dane grinned sheepishly. "You could say that."

He glanced around the room, an idea forming. "Roxanne, can you do me a favor and find a way to position yourself near his table, so I can look at you when I hold my phone up?"

Roxanne looked at him sideways, arching a brow. "Sure, but why?"

"I want to get a picture, so I can have Jake run it through his facial recognition program. I'm pretty sure Seth isn't really named Seth. It'd be easier to prove that if we got a decent picture."

Roxanne nodded. "Oh, right. On my way." She grabbed a pot of coffee and began weaving her way through tables with refills.

***

Chloe parked her borrowed car in front of Roxanne's store. Her heart was brimming. She was so excited to have made the decision to stay in Catamount that she was silly with joy. There was, of course, the thrill in her heart and body whenever she thought of Dane, but it ran deeper than that. When she'd started on her hike so many months ago in late spring in the already sweltering heat of Georgia, it had felt like stepping off a cliff. For her, it was in so many ways. Every decision in her life up to that point hadn't required much thought. She simply did what she thought she was supposed to do—get good grades, go to a good college, get a business degree, fall in love with a nice young man, get engaged and eventually get married. She'd made it through every phase but the getting married part without ever really *thinking* about what she genuinely wanted. Perhaps, she wouldn't have known the answer, but she'd never stopped to question.

By nature, she was an obedient girl. She'd taken a look at her parents and done what she thought they wanted. Since the events unfolded in her life and she'd left Tom, quit her job and made plans to hike the Appalachian Trail, her mother had surprised her with her unwavering support. Oh, she'd been taken aback at points, but she'd handled it all in stride. Chloe had come to realize her mother just wanted her to live a fulfilling life, regardless of the path she took to get there.

Meeting Dane in that shadowed cave, feeling the electricity arc between them, she'd been drawn to look inside herself in a way she hadn't before. She shook her head as she recalled the night he'd shown her he was a mountain lion shifter. He hadn't shifted in her presence again, and she wanted to ask him about it. Now that she'd had a few weeks to adjust to the knowledge and understand it, she wanted to see it free from the haze of surprise. For now though, she wanted a cup of coffee from Roxanne's and perhaps one of her amazing sandwiches. Dane was at work and would be until this evening. Chloe still had to figure out what she would do for work, but for now—coffee.

Shana had loaned her car to Chloe, insisting she could hitch rides from friends when needed. Thinking of Shana made her heart clench. Chloe was just starting to get to know her, but it was clear she was devastated by Callen's death. Now that Chloe had experienced the depth of feeling she had for Dane, she could imagine the despair she'd feel if something happened to him.

She climbed out of Shana's car and paused to look around. A brisk fall wind blew through the air. The manicured town green was dusted in the harvest confetti of fall leaves. Dane had told her to expect snow to fly any day now. Thanksgiving was right around the corner. She'd promised her mother a visit for the New Year with plans to bring Dane with her, but she wanted to spend Thanksgiving here. She felt it would anchor her to Catamount, the connection, the celebration of harvest and settling in for winter.

Tugging her jacket around her, she walked up the steps to Roxanne's grateful for the burst of warmth from the bustling store when she entered. After getting her coffee and enjoying a sandwich, she walked back outside and decided to take a short walk around the green. The homes that lined the green were labeled with tastefully painted signs indicating when the homes were built and the original owners. In the back of her mind, she held Dane's warning to be alert, but she couldn't imagine she'd be anything but safe here in the center of town with stores lining the green and people strolling on the sidewalks.

The wind chilled her as she walked, but she enjoyed the fact that she could walk almost without a limp now. Her sprained ankle was close to feeling normal. She thought perhaps she'd ask Dane to join her to finish the tail end of the Appalachian Trail next spring. It wasn't wise to try now with her ankle so freshly healed and winter nipping at the air. As she walked along the sidewalk, passing a narrow alley between two old buildings, she felt a hand wrap around her arm. Before she could make a sound, another hand clapped over her mouth and she was thrown into the back seat of a vehicle. As soon as the door slammed shut, the vehicle began moving. Chloe looked up to see Seth, the man who'd acted as if he knew Dane, glancing back at her.

***

Dane saw his last patient of the day out the door and locked it. His receptionist had already left for the day. He did a quick walk through of the office, switching off computers and lights as he moved through. He tried calling Chloe once again, puzzled she hadn't replied to any of his texts or answered his calls. He'd come to learn she wasn't one to be coy and hold off on answering calls or texts, often replying within minutes. So her silence was unusual and making him uneasy. Seeing that Roxanne had called him, he moved to return the call when another call came in as he walked to his truck.

"Dane here," he said quickly.

"Get over here as soon as you can," Jake barked in his ear.

"Just leaving the office, I'll be right there. What's up?"

He heard Jake's deep breath, his gut kicking into gear at the sound.

"Roxanne said that Gail Anderson came running over to tell her she saw Chloe get dragged into some car and driven away."

Jake's words hit Dane like a blow. His breath was gone, his heart in his throat. His tires squealed as he raced the two blocks to Jake's office and came to a screeching stop.

Barreling through the door, he pocketed his phone and stared at Jake. "Why the hell didn't somebody call me sooner?" he all but shouted. His lion rolled under his skin, clawing to come out and attack whoever had Chloe.

Jake didn't flinch. "Roxanne said she tried to call you, but you didn't answer. So she called me. Bless Gail's heart. Even though she's pushing eighty, her eyes are sharp. She got the license plate number. Roxanne said Gail didn't have a clue as to the car make and model, but said it was a black sports vehicle. While I was calling you, I looked it up. I also ran Seth's photo through the system earlier today and planned to call you about that. He's not only lying about his name, but he's got a hell of a background issue. The license plate links to a rental car company, so I'm hacking into their system to see who rented the car. I'm thinking I sit tight for a few and get this sorted out while you head out and look for the vehicle. Roxanne said she'd round up anyone else she can to help look. Don't worry about stopping to talk with her, she said to tell you she's got it covered and will send everyone out with all the info I get to her."

Dane could barely catch his breath. Fear for Chloe raced through him. He closed his eyes and held still, trying to keep his lion in check. He couldn't drive in lion form, he needed to keep it together. He opened his eyes and met Jake's concerned and angry gaze.

"Go," Jake said simply.

"Okay, call me with anything you find."

He turned and left, tearing out of the parking lot. He made a quick call to Roxanne to ask her to assign people to different sections of town.

Chapter 11

Chloe batted back the fear that raced through her. Seth was in the passenger seat and occasionally glanced her way, but had said little since they began driving. A man she'd seen somewhere around town was driving. She wracked her brain trying to recall where she'd seen him. He was silent as he drove down a dirt road in the forest, coming to a stop in front of a small cabin.

Seth turned to her. "Here's the deal, we don't want to hurt you. We have some business with Dane, and unfortunately, we needed some leverage."

"I'm leverage?" she asked, fury and fear warring inside of her.

Seth shrugged. "Yup. You mean a lot to Dane, so you're our best option." He opened the car door, following the driver outside of the car. They conferred briefly by the steps of the cabin. Chloe strained to hear them, but their voices were muffled. Leaves blew in a swirl around the car. The driver walked into the cabin and Seth came to the car, opening the door at her side.

He looked at her carefully, his gray eyes neutral.

"Don't try anything. If you've seen Dane shift, you know what we can do."

Chloe didn't bother to nod and refused to reply. But she wasn't stupid either, so she followed him when he escorted her out of the car and into the small cabin. She glanced around when she got inside. It appeared to be a hunting cabin—sparsely furnished, a basic kitchen, one large room with simple furniture and a bathroom and bedroom off to the side.

The driver entered the cabin from a door at the back with an armful of wood. He nodded at Chloe, but was otherwise silent. She suddenly realized where she's seen him—at Roxanne's. He'd been pointed out as Callen's younger brother, but she didn't actually meet him and didn't know his name.

"You're Callen's brother," she said.

The man's head whipped up. He had gray eyes, like many shifters. His hair didn't have the warm, golden hue of Dane's, but was a flat, dark blonde. His eyes sharpened on her and then bounced to Seth.

"I thought you said she didn't know who I was," the man stated.

Seth glanced between them, his gaze calculating. "I didn't think she did. She's pretty new to town, according to you." Seth's words held a return accusation.

"What's your name?" Chloe asked. "I know who you are, so you might as well tell me your name."

The man shook his head. "Nope. Callen has more than one brother. I'll let you wonder on that."

Chloe's brain whirred, recalling Dane's concerns about what had happened to Callen. Though she was far from clear on any details, it was obvious that this brother of his may have something to do with whatever Dane was worried about. Interesting that Callen's brother didn't want her to know who he was. He obviously had plenty to hide. If only she could piece together what they wanted from Dane.

The man ignored her and went to place the wood in a rack by a small woodstove. He quickly built a fire. Seth gestured for her to sit in a chair in the corner, so she did. The wheels in her mind spun, wondering when Dane would realize she was gone and how she could help if someone found her out here. She surreptitiously studied the room, but it was sparse enough there wasn't much to help her. She figured she simply needed to be ready if and when Dane, or anyone, came to help. In the meantime, she'd try to stay quiet and see if they let anything slip.

Seth stepped outside a few times to make calls while Callen's brother remained silent for the most part. He pulled out a laptop. They'd taken her phone once she'd been thrown in the car. But they didn't know her watch was synced to her phone and had its own GPS. She prayed the GPS locator would work out here.

***

Dane drove wildly along the winding road toward the area where Jake said Chloe's watch was pinging a signal. "How do you know it's her watch?" Dane asked.

"Because it's identifier says so. You must have noticed she had one of those fancy watches that tracks her fitness and what not," Jake retorted.

"I noticed. Guess I didn't know it had its own GPS signal."

Jake shrugged. "Sure does. Lucky she has it. It's synced to her phone, so when I tried to look up her phone and got no signal, the information indicated her watch was linked. I'm guessing they had her turn over her phone and didn't think to check on anything else."

Jake had assigned his younger sister, Liliana, to stay at his office and monitor the signal. He rode in the passenger seat of Dane's truck. Cold fury and hot fear warred within Dane. He was beyond angry with Seth and whoever else was behind Chloe's kidnapping and terrified for her safety. Jake had confirmed what they suspected. Seth's legal name wasn't Seth, but Steven Meyer. Jake had chased down his driver's license to Montana in a small town outside of Bozeman. He had a list of petty crimes tagged to his legal name, but nothing that came close to kidnapping, mostly minor drug offenses. Dane's mind spun with fears for Chloe's safety and how to make sure they got her safe.

Jake rode beside him silently, his anger pulsing like a force with Dane's. Jake feared for Chloe, as Dane did, but he didn't have the emotion tied to her. He'd stewed over why they'd kidnapped Chloe, circling back again and again to the idea that they needed her for leverage to get to Dane.

"Whatever we do, we try to keep them alive, so we can find out what the hell they want with us," Jake said flatly.

Though neither Dane, nor Jake, had ever considered the possibility they may kill someone, they both knew there was a high likelihood they would shift into lion form to do whatever was necessary to get Chloe safe. All bets were off if they happened to be facing another shifter or more.

Jake's phone buzzed in the quiet truck. He answered quickly. "Jake here."

"Uh huh, okay no movement then? Any other news?"

Dane heard the muffled sounds of a response and waited until Jake hung up.

"What's up?" he asked sharply.

"Liliana called like I asked to update us that the

GPS signal for Chloe's watch is still in the same place. She's keeping herself busy trying to hack into Seth's computer, or the computer she traced to the address listed on his driver's license. She also pulled up his phone records and is seeing if she can trace his GPS signal too. That's all assuming that what we traced to his legal name actually belongs to him."

Dane nodded. "Right, well based on the coordinates you gave me, we should be coming up on the location any minute now. You aware of any cabins out this way?"

They'd headed out of Catamount, following the main highway that traveled through town and off onto a smaller highway and onto a dirt road he presumed was a logging road. There were miles and miles of logging roads crisscrossing the Maine woods, some in active use by logging companies, others mostly used by locals for travel into the woods. Having grown up in Catamount, Dane was familiar with the areas where families had camps and hunting cabins. This road was unknown to him.

Jake checked his phone. "Stop for a sec and cut the lights" he said.

Dane braked abruptly, flicking the lights off immediately. Jake checked the coordinates on his phone and those Liliana had texted him. He pointed ahead into the dark. The GPS locator should be no more than half a mile away. If someone's out here, we need to slow down and move without your lights, so they don't see us coming."

Dane nodded and waited in the dark for his eyes to adjust. Without the glare of headlights, it took a moment before he could see the road stretching ahead of them in the dark. As he looked ahead, he saw a flickering light through the trees that he likely wouldn't have seen with the headlights on.

He pointed without a word. Jake nodded as soon as

he saw the light through the trees. "Get as close as you can staying on the main road here. Looks like the cabin is off another road. We don't want to get blocked in, so let's park and walk."

Dane rolled the truck along slowly until they reached what appeared to be a driveway leading to the small cabin they could barely see through the trees. With only the light flickering in the windows, they walked silently through the woods, circling around to the back of the cabin. The light they saw came from a fire in a woodstove. Otherwise, not a single light was on. Dane had never seen this cabin. It was on the newer side, likely built within the last few years. The Maine woods were filled with family hunting cabins, many old and weathered. The newness of the cabin gave him pause. He couldn't help but wonder how Seth knew of this place and what it meant about who might be helping him. It had to be someone from Catamount to have guided him to a cabin in an undisclosed location in the well-traveled woods of this area. The vein of forest threaded by the Appalachian Trail was a heavily trafficked area of wilderness. Somehow they'd managed to find a location outside the radar of the commonly traversed areas.

Dane hated the sense of distrust he felt ever since Jake had broken the news about Callen. Much as he wanted to believe Callen had acted alone, his gut told him otherwise.

He and Jake had agreed they wouldn't shift before they entered the cabin. They both strongly suspected Seth was a shifter himself, but they didn't want to reveal themselves unless it was necessary. They walked quietly toward the cabin. When they reached the back wall and could access a window, Dane moved with silence and precision, carefully checking the window and sliding it open. A whisper of sound came with the flow of cold air entering the room.

They waited in the quiet dark, voices filtering out to them. Two men were speaking. Dane and Jake glanced at each other when they simultaneously recognized one of the voices. Dane's mind grasped for whose it was. He knew the voice without a doubt, but he couldn't say whom it belonged to. Jake shook his head and shrugged. Jake climbed through the window first. Only after he was inside and held still for a long moment did he gesture for Dane to move around to the front. They'd agreed one would enter from the back and the other the front. Dane moved swiftly, waiting quietly by the front door. He would punch through an adjacent window to open it if it turned out to be locked. He didn't plan to test the knob in case they saw it move. As soon as he heard a chair scrape across the floor, he plunged through the door.

As he did, his eyes landed on Chloe seated in a chair in the corner, her hands free and her eyes wide. Any plans to stay calm flew out of his mind, primal instinct taking over. His fierce desire to protect her welled, and he let his cat loose, shifting instantly. As his eyes scanned the room, he saw Callen's youngest brother, Randall, who shifted the moment he saw Dane. In the span of a breath, all four men shifted into lion form.

Chapter 12

Chloe saw Jake before Seth and the other man did. He held a finger to his lips, his eyes coasting over her in the shadowy room, appearing to check if she was okay. She didn't dare nod, but tried to convey with her eyes that she was okay. She was okay in the basic sense of the word, but she was wired and exhausted at once. Angry and frightened, her anxiety driven higher by the hours of near silent tension in the cabin. The moment she saw Jake, she knew Dane had to be nearby. Her breath caught, the sense of relief was so immense. She'd known he would be looking for her, but she hadn't known how afraid she was that he might not find her. She still hadn't been able to get much information from the snippets of conversations she'd overheard. When the two men were in the front room with her, they spoke casually if they spoke at all, of nothing related to why they needed leverage against Dane.

Suddenly, the man with Seth stiffened. Without a word, he stood abruptly, his chair scraping loudly against the floor. The front door flung open in a blur. For a split second, Chloe saw Dane, his blue-gray eyes caressing her.

In another second, all four men shifted. She was surrounded by mountain lions, all with hair raised on their backs and tails swishing. Dane hissed, baring his teeth. He and Jake were roughly equal in size, both larger than Seth and Callen's brother. Chloe knew she should be more frightened, but the sight was so stunning, she was in awe. Seeing Dane in his glory as a lion was breathtaking. He ignored Callen's brother completely, his dominance apparent over the other lion. Dane and Jake met eyes, the air fairly crackling between them. Jake turned to Callen's brother and with a snarl, swiped at him, chasing him out of the cabin.

Dane turned to Seth, who was much slighter than Dane. Dane was all muscle and sinewy motion. He leapt across the room, backing Seth into a corner, snarling and roaring. Seth evaded Dane's swipes and managed to slide over by the door and slip out. Dane's haunches bunched in a leap as he followed Seth out the door. Chloe flew out of her chair and raced to the door, flicking on the outside light.

The lions were a blur of motion, gold flashing in and out of the light. Jake and Callen's brother alternated with swipes and snarling. Seth dashed into the woods, Dane following, his motion near silent though its power was stunning. He stalked Seth through the trees, winding in between them and leaping off of them. He climbed into the branches of an oak tree, waiting silently while Seth glanced over his shoulder to find him. When Seth circled under the tree, Dane leapt onto his back. They rolled into the clearing again, a bundle of claws and fur.

Chloe's heart raced, fear nearly choking her, when Callen's brother broke away from Jake and joined Seth in his battle with Dane. Before Jake could reach them, Callen's brother and Seth, whom Chloe could only identify by size, managed to pin Dane to the ground. Blood streaked his fur where they tore at him. Without thinking, Chloe moved toward them, thinking she had to find a way to help, only to freeze when Dane roared in her direction.

Chloe had lost sight of Jake and worried he'd gone, only to see that he'd circled behind the cluster. He waited silently in the trees, his eyes locked on the other cats. When the moment was right, he leapt forward with a snarl and knocked Callen's brother away. This afforded Dane the opportunity to regain control over Seth. With a swipe, Dane flung Seth against a tree, stunning him momentarily. Seth fell to the ground. Dane stood above him and roared, the sound echoing through the dark woods. Dane leaned forward and bit into Seth's neck, the fur streaking with blood under the grip of Dane's teeth. Seth struggled against Dane's grip before going limp and rolling over in submission. Dane gave a shake with his teeth before slowly releasing him. Jake had pinned Callen's brother under his paw, leaving him close to limp at this point.

Chloe's heart was galloping. The wild, primal sight of these lions fighting and establishing who had the most power was unlike anything she'd ever witnessed, or even imagined witnessing. Watching Dane standing silent in the woods, her fear subsided and intense desire rose within her. She didn't realize she'd been holding her breath until she saw Seth and Callen's brother shift into human form again. Their bodies retained the scratches and bite marks from the skirmish with Jake and Dane. The men remained where they'd been pinned, naked and injured. Jake and Dane waited a beat and shifted back into human form themselves.

Chloe suddenly realized she was staring at four naked men. She glanced behind her into the cabin and saw four sets of clothes in rumpled piles on the floor where they'd shifted. She gathered them up, noticing most of the clothes were torn. She figured they'd have to make do. She carried the clothes out to them, her heart thudding. Adrenaline raced through her from the fear of the afternoon and evening, along with the thrill of watching Dane and Jake subdue the two men who'd intended to use her for leverage. Dane didn't move from where he stood by Seth. He turned his head and met her eyes, his blue-gray eyes glowing, intense and otherworldly, in the dark woods. He silently accepted the clothes she offered and threw some on top of Seth.

Chloe walked over to Jake and handed him the other pairs of clothes. Moments later, all four men were clothed, albeit in tattered outfits. Dane and Jake escorted the two men back into the cabin. Chloe wondered if it was safe not to tie them up, but she sensed Dane and Jake had it in hand. Dane dragged another chair beside the one where she'd been sitting and gestured for the two men to sit.

Jake stood at Dane's side, both men bristling with energy and fury. Dane ignored Seth and looked at Callen's brother. "So Randall, looks like you were in cahoots with Callen?"

Randall whipped his head up, clearly taken off guard at Dane's question. His eyes bounced between Jake and Dane. They remained silent. "Don't know what you're talking about," Randall said flatly.

Dane leaned forward, his face inches from Randall's. "I think you do. If you were hoping to use Chloe against me, you miscalculated how much leverage we have against you. We won't fill you in, we'll let you wonder about that. But know this: we are well aware Callen planned to sell Catamount shifters out. We have no problem bringing shame down on your entire family. And this…" Dane gestured around the room. "This little hidden cabin and your kidnapping plan of *my* fiancée…this won't fly. You'll pay and fast."

Chloe's heart hammered against her ribs. The way Dane spoke about her, his fierceness and intensity, sent a thrill humming through her body. His eyes met hers briefly, electricity snapped between them. Had they been alone, Chloe would have fallen into his arms. She forced herself to stay still though her body practically vibrated.

Randall's face went white, but he remained silent, his expression sullen. Dane glanced to Chloe again, his eyes briefly caressing her. Without even touching her, she felt a wave of comfort wash from him. He looked back at Randall and over to Seth.

"So here's the deal. Half the town's out looking for Chloe. We've already arranged for the police to head our way once Jake signaled Liliana that we located the cabin. They shouldn't be more than a few minutes behind us. In the meantime, you can sit tight and shut up, or consider whether you want to tell us what you can to see if you might earn a lesser punishment."

Randall looked at Seth, his eyes traveling to Jake and landing on Dane. He shook his head. "Fuck you."

Lights flashed through the trees as a car turned down the road leading to the cabin, more lights following behind. The next few hours were a jumble in Chloe's mind. The Catamount police arrived and promptly arrested Randall and Seth. Chloe rode back into town with Dane and Jake, held snug against Dane's side. They hadn't had even a second of privacy, so Chloe made do with a quick kiss and Dane's strong arm around her while adrenaline and emotion surged through her. Between the fear she'd experienced for her own circumstances, she'd been terrified Dane would be hurt during the altercation with Randall. Watching four shifters in lion form had been thrilling and ethereal, but it was frightening to know that Dane or Jake could have been hurt.

A number of residents were waiting at the police station when they arrived. Word had traveled like brushfire. Chloe was taken aside for questioning, along with Dane and Jake. When she was waiting outside for Dane to finish up, she was pestered with questions from residents. People were shocked and confused about Randall's involvement. Roxanne arrived and waved everyone away from Chloe. "For God's sake people, give her some space. I know we're all scared and concerned, but give it some time. The police will give us more information once they've sorted everything out."

Chloe breathed a sigh of relief when the pressure of questions was eased. "Thank you," she said under her breath.

Roxanne shrugged. "No problem. People are flat freaking out. I get it. I am too, but badgering you for answers isn't going to help. You okay?"

Chloe nodded. She was tired, weary, and crashing from the after-effects of hours of fear and adrenaline pumping through her body. "I'm okay. Tired and ready to go home though."

She felt a hand on her shoulder and knew it was Dane's the moment he touched her. His palm slid down her back in a smooth caress, coming to rest at her waist. Warmth stole through her, his touch soothing and electrifying at once. "Well, that's good then because that's where we're going."

He stepped to her side, smiling down at her, his blue-gray eyes coasting over her.

"Hey Roxanne, thanks for waiting with Chloe," he added.

Roxanne looked at him, her expression somber. "Of course. I won't bother you about it now, but I don't suppose you could fill me in tomorrow?"

Dane nodded. "You got it. I'll stop by in the morning."

Chapter 13

Dane walked beside Chloe into the house, his hand on her back. He couldn't keep from touching her on the way home. It was as if he needed to reassure himself she was physically here with him. The events of the afternoon and evening were fresh in his mind. The pounding fear he'd felt had barely abated. The thought of what could have happened if they hadn't found her terrified him. Anger at Randall, Seth, and whoever else lay behind her kidnapping simmered inside. There was a lot left to deal with, but for now, he simply needed to be with Chloe.

As soon as the door closed behind them, he picked her up in his arms and walked upstairs. Her mossy green eyes met his in the shadowed hall, intent and focused. He carried her through the bedroom and into the bathroom before setting her down. "We're washing today off of you," he said as he reached in and turned on the shower.

In seconds, steam began to filter through the room. Chloe had immediately begun taking her clothes off. Dane stripped his tattered clothes off, following her into the shower. Soft light fell through the haze of water and steam.

The glass blue tiles created a surreal space around them. He pulled her into his arms and simply held her, the heat of the water rushing over them. He had to force himself to step back. Lust streaked through him, its force primal. He soaped her, savoring the feel of her soft skin and curves under his hands. While she rinsed off under the water and lathered her hair with shampoo, he washed himself quickly. Bubbles ran over her body as she rinsed her hair. His cock throbbed at the sight of her.

He reached for her again when she opened her eyes, her lashes spiked with water, the green of her eyes bright. Her tongue darted out, licking a drop of water. He couldn't hold back and took her mouth in a deep kiss, instantly delving in with his tongue. She met him stroke for stroke, their kiss wild, hot and deep. The coils of want tightened in him. After the fight tonight and his shift, he'd barely been able to keep his primal desire for her in check. To have her here, naked in his arms, unleashed everything he'd been holding back.

***

Dane's kiss was fierce, his energy potent. A frisson of awareness unrolled in a stretch through Chloe's body. Desire raged inside of her. He lifted her against him, cupping her bottom in his strong hands. Her legs went around his waist as he stepped to the wall of the shower, bringing her back against it. He pressed against her, his arousal resting in the cradle of her hips, directly against her cleft. Pleasure pin-wheeled through her when he rocked into her, nestling against the nub of her desire.

The afternoon of pulses of fear, hours of dread and waiting, and then the crash of adrenaline when Dane and Jake fought Seth and Randall culminated in this. The primal beauty of witnessing Dane shift into his lion and *be* who and what he was had been so intense, she'd barely held it together since then. The emotional intensity of feeling safe and so protected by him was unlike anything she'd ever experienced, or could have imagined. She needed to slake the depth of her feelings against the flint of the conflagration between them.

He tore his lips away, murmuring her name as he kissed his way down her neck, his lips closing over a nipple. She arched into him with a cry when he bit her softly and swirled his tongue around. He did the same with her other nipple. She shifted restlessly against him, grinding her hips into the warm length of his cock. She needed him inside of her.

He lifted his head, stroking the wet strands of her hair away from her face. She met his eyes, that blue-gray gaze so intense, solely focused on her. Holding her eyes, he shifted back and brought the head of his cock to her entrance, slowing dragging it through her wet folds. She moaned, biting her lip to keep from shattering too soon. In a swift surge, he filled her to the hilt, settling against her, his hard muscled chest flush against her breasts. The contrast of his heated body with the cool tiles on her back ratcheted up her desire. He held still for a long moment, lifting a hand and stroking it down her cheek. It came to rest in the curve of her neck, his thumb at the beat of her pulse.

He began a cycle of slow, deep strokes, holding her firmly against him, the strength of his hold never wavering. She came in a noisy burst, flying apart in his arms. He followed her, convulsing within her. His forehead fell to hers. Their breath mingled with the steam and water falling around them.

They toweled off and fell into bed, no words passing between them. Dane tucked her against his body, the quilt cocooning them.

Chloe woke the next morning, curled against Dane's warmth. He lay on his back, his head resting on one elbow, his other hand moving in slow circles on her back.

"It snowed last night." His voice was gravelly from sleep.

He turned his head to meet her eyes. She leaned up and landed a soft kiss on his lips before resting her head on his chest to look out the window. A large picture window in his bedroom faced a field with woods behind it. Everything was dusted in the lightest coat of snow, as if fairy dust had been sprinkled during the night.

Chapter 14

Dane leaned his hips against Jake's desk, his arms crossed, and listened. Jake and Hank Anderson, the police chief for Catamount, were discussing Jake's online investigation of Callen.

Hank shook his head. "Damn, this is a hell of a mess. Callen put us at some serious risk. Seth and Randall aren't talking. If you ask me, Randall is in way over his head. I'm with Jake on Callen, though. Wouldn't put it past him. I know it's devastating for his family, and Shana," he said, pausing with a glance at Dane.

Dane shook his head, his jaw tight. Shana was holed up at Phoebe's. When he stopped by this morning, her eyes were so puffy from crying, he didn't have the heart to try to talk further about it. He hugged her and left her in Phoebe's comforting presence.

Hank continued. "So let me see if I have this right: Callen's been in contact with someone out West who's back and forth between Montana and South Dakota. Callen proposed his plan to offer up shifters to smuggle drugs for major money. We have no names, but we managed to trace

Seth's computer fingerprints back to Montana. Obviously, whomever Callen was in touch with traced him back to Catamount. Randall's in on it, but I get the sense he doesn't know everything behind the scenes. Randall was always dogging Callen's footsteps, trying to prove himself. Callen knew he had an easy sell with Randall. Seth has more knowledge. I can sense it. The only good thing to come out of Chloe's kidnapping is I have solid felony charges to hold them."

Dane felt the lion within him prickle and rise, his fury at Chloe's kidnapping was alive and well. He was keeping a lid on it, but what he wanted was to set his lion loose and tear Seth and Randall to pieces. But the human in him knew that wouldn't get them any answers, nor would it guarantee Chloe's safety. He forced himself to focus on the discussion at hand. With the layers of risks Catamount shifters were facing because of Callen, Dane was relieved to have Hank working on the investigation. Hank was another shifter, so he knew how to navigate the legal waters without drawing attention to shifter rumors.

"So will you be able to use what Jake found?" Dane asked.

Hank chuckled. "Hell yeah!" He turned and caught Jake's eyes. "Good thing is you're not bound by stuff like warrants. You can find whatever you want and turn it over to me."

Jake nodded. "So what now?"

"Now we wait and let the wheels start moving in slow motion in the legal system. On the one hand, that'll buy us some time. But on the other, I don't know who else might be sent our way after this," Hank replied, his gaze somber. "I'm damn glad both of you are stronger and faster than they were. If we come up against some shifters that are much bigger, it might not work out so well. I've got my guys developing plans for how to monitor around town. I'm hoping once they get word their plan didn't work out, that whoever else is behind this will avoid making any more moves."

Dane's mind flashed back to the sight of Chloe in the corner of the cabin, alone and frightened. He recalled the report that she'd been dragged into the car. He wasn't sure if it was better or worse that he hadn't witnessed it. His imagination had gone wild with pictures of it. Chloe insisted they didn't physically harm her. His stomach coiled with fury at how they described her as 'leverage'. With a sharp shake of his head, he brought his focus back to Jake and Hank.

"Keep me posted and let me know what else I can help with." Dane glanced out the window. It was early evening and the light had faded. Around the town green, holiday lights sparkled. In another week, it would be Thanksgiving. "I gotta head over to Roxanne's to pick up Chloe. Catch you guys later." He gave a quick wave and strode out to his truck.

Moments later, he pulled up across the street from Roxanne's store. Chloe had spent the morning at his office. Even though Seth and Randall were sitting in jail, he wasn't comfortable having her stay alone anywhere right now. He'd quickly discovered she didn't enjoy being idle. She'd helped his receptionist, Jackie, handle most of the filing. After they had lunch at Roxanne's, Roxanne promised to keep her busy for the afternoon.

As he walked toward the store, a bracing gust of wind hit him. Fall leaves swirled in the air, scudding across the street. The light snow from last night had melted during the day, but winter was firmly on its way. He expected a decent amount of snowfall in the next few weeks.

Stepping inside Roxanne's, he breathed deeply.

Roxanne had a brick oven for baking in the back, which generated a lot of heat, along with filling the entire store with the scent of fresh-baked bread. He threaded his way through the aisles and found Chloe seated at a table with a cup of coffee and her laptop. She met his eyes with a smile, those mossy green eyes of hers pulling at him. He gave her what was meant to be a quick kiss, but morphed into a deep, sensual, breath-stealing kiss. Her tongue coasted across the seam of his lips, immediately tangling with his when he opened his mouth. He cupped her cheek, his thumb brushing across her pulse.

The sound of a throat clearing nearby snapped him into focus. He pulled away reluctantly to find Roxanne standing by the table with a cup of coffee in hand for him. "I try to provide fast service, and you're about to throw her on the table." Roxanne clucked and shook her head. The pen so often tucked behind her ear slipped out and clattered to the floor.

Dane bent over and picked it up, handing it to her with a sheepish smile. "Can't help myself. Thanks for the coffee," he replied, accepting it from her and sitting down across from Chloe.

"You can kiss her anytime you want, just don't make it R-rated in here," Roxanne said. She glanced to Chloe. "Did you tell him?"

Dane looked at Chloe. "Tell me what?"

"I figured out what I can do for work! Roxanne says Catamount could use another accountant. That's right up my alley since I got my degree in business and accounting. But that's not all I want to do, but it'll keep me busy. Once I've got enough clients to keep me afloat, I'm going to open my own clothing store. I always wanted to start my own business, but figured it wasn't a safe decision this early. Between the accounting and the much more affordable rents around here, I'll be able to get something going." Chloe's eyes were glowing.

Dane was pleased because he knew she wouldn't be content to stay in Catamount without establishing herself independently. He grinned and lifted his coffee mug in a mock toast. "Perfect! You can start with my accounts."

Roxanne grinned and walked off. Dane looked over at Chloe, his eyes sobering. "I've noticed you don't like lounging around, so it's good to hear you've already figured something out."

Chloe shrugged sheepishly. "I don't do bored well." She paused, her eyes narrowing on him. "Did you talk to the police chief?"

"Yup. He's got plenty to work with from Jake's online snooping. In the meantime, he'll be able to hold Seth and Randall on felony charges for the kidnapping, so you won't need to worry about that. In the meantime, we wait. I'm sure you've noticed most of the town is freaking out. The news about Callen is ugly."

Chloe nodded soberly. "I know. I wish we knew everything, like who was behind it, who Callen knew and so on. He put all of the shifters here at risk. It scares me we don't know more yet."

Dane's throat tightened at her words. He hadn't doubted she planned to stay in Catamount, but to hear her concern meant more than he could say. She'd accepted him and the other shifters—their safety, and by extension, their very future, mattered to her. He met her eyes, bringing his focus to the moment again.

"You and me both. We're working on it. In the meantime, we haven't talked about it, but I'm wondering what your plans are for Thanksgiving? I'm hoping you'll stay here, but I know you might want to go visit your family." He reached across the table and grasped her hand, rubbing his thumb across the back of it.

She smiled softly. "I was planning to ask you. I mean, I'm here now and I'm not going anywhere, but I didn't know what you usually did at the holidays. I thought maybe we could have Thanksgiving here, and I could take you to meet my family later."

Dane's heart thudded against his ribcage, the lion inside him purring. The idea of having her here with him during a time that represented family and blessings meant so much, his heart clenched. He smiled at her. "Sounds great."

When they walked outside a few minutes later, snow was falling softly. Giant flakes fluttered down from the sky, sparkling in the streetlights.

Epilogue

Chloe walked across the street to Roxanne's store. Snow blanketed the ground. A few lingering bright fall leaves swirled in the air, dotting the snow with splashes of color. As she walked up the stairs to the door, it swung open, Roxanne's smiling face behind it.

"Hey there, you're early. Let me get that," Roxanne said, removing a warm casserole pan from Chloe's hands.

Dane had explained that even before his parents passed away, they usually spent Thanksgiving dinner at Roxanne's store with a few other local families. The tradition had been established before this generation, but it continued without interruption. Dane was meeting her here after a quick stop at his office to set a broken arm for a little boy who thought riding his bike on the icy street was a good idea this morning.

Chloe followed Roxanne into the store, weaving her way through the aisles. When she reached the deli and coffee shop area, she discovered it had been transformed. The small round tables had been stacked against the wall and two long tables had been pushed together with enough seating for over twenty people. The entire store was scented with delicious food. Roxanne quickly set Chloe to work ladling fresh brewed hard cider and slicing loaves of herbed breads as Roxanne pulled them out of the oven.

Within the hour, the area was filled with people. Chloe had met most of them. Roxanne made sure she was introduced to anyone she didn't already know. Chloe thought back over the last month and found it hard to believe she felt so at home in Catamount. She simply did and didn't care to question it. When she was with Dane, her heart thrummed with joy and desire every moment. As she'd known that evening in the woods when he found her in the cave, the connection between them was so powerful, it spoke for itself. The community had gone from being polite and somewhat reserved to welcoming her with open arms. The aftermath of the kidnapping lingered in town and within her, but the event seemed to have brought the community to rally around her. The shifters knew she accepted them.

The only blot on her happiness was the undercurrent of fear and sadness around Callen, his death, and what the town had since learned about him. Betrayal and fear ran high when his name came up. Chloe had a few opportunities to spend time with Shana and felt deeply for her. Though she couldn't say she understood Shana's experience entirely, she understood what it was like to find out someone you trusted was not the person you believed them to be. She hoped for Shana's sake that she would find a way past it. As for the shifters, the investigation continued into who else was behind Callen's planning. Dane kept her up to date and had explained the investigation had tentacles reaching from Maine to South Dakota and Montana. Time would tell what they learned.

Chloe glanced up when she heard her name. Dane

was weaving his way through the room to her side. The faint scent of wood smoke clung to him. She leaned up to kiss him, flushing when he pulled her close and swept his tongue into her mouth. He never did anything halfway, and one kiss took her breath away.

"How many times do I have to remind you to take it easy?" Roxanne's question broke through the haze of passion.

Chloe flushed when Dane pulled away. Dane shrugged with a grin, entirely unrepentant. "I'd say I was sorry, but I'm not."

Roxanne swatted him on the shoulder. "Be glad I like her, or I might make it much more awkward for you."

The next few hours passed in a blur of food, wine, cider, and an overwhelming sense of belonging. After Thanksgiving dinner had been served and everyone stuffed beyond reason, Chloe rode beside Dane as he drove home through the quiet night. Leaves blew across the road in the path of his headlights. When they walked inside, Dane started a fire in the fireplace in his bedroom. Chloe sat on the small couch by the fire, her legs resting across Dane's lap.

He turned to her, his blue-gray eyes intent on her. Holding her gaze, he reached for a small wooden box sitting on the table beside the couch. He held it in his palm, his eyes pinned to hers. "I knew it the night I met you. There is no one for me but you. I considered waiting, but I don't want there to be any question about my intent. If you tell me you're not ready, I'll wait."

He handed her the box, warm from his touch. Her heart beat wildly—joy and anticipation laced with uncertainty flashed through her. The box was old, the wood a deep, rich brown. Carvings covered its surface. She held it closer and saw intricate carvings of mountain lions on every face of the box. She lifted the lid and gasped. A gorgeous ring set with emeralds and diamonds was nestled inside.

Her eyes flew to Dane's. For the first time ever, she saw the slightest hint of uncertainty in the depths of his gaze. "I chose the emerald because it reminds me of your eyes."

"Oh, oh…" Tears sprang to her eyes. Her mind went wild for a split second, the planner in her ready to point out how rash it would be to agree marry Dane so soon. But her heart knew the truth and calmly told her mind to stop worrying unnecessarily.

"There's no need to wait," she said simply.

Dane's breath came out in a rush. He tugged her onto his lap. "Even though I've known you were meant for me the moment I met you, I didn't know what to do if you weren't sure. I'd have waited…"

Chloe's heart flew with joy, so full she could barely contain the feeling. She cut his words off with a soft kiss. "But you don't need to."

Dane's forehead fell to hers, his lips landing on hers in the softest of kisses.

~The End~

Please enjoy the following excerpt from **Chosen Mate**, the next book in the Catamount Lion Shifters Series!

Protected Mate (Catamount Lion Shifters)

Chapter 1

Jake North woke with a jump when the door to his office opened. "Huh?" he said groggily.

"Seriously, Jake? Did you sleep here last night?"

Jake rubbed his eyes and ran a hand through his hair, looking up to find Phoebe Devine standing beside his desk.

"I guess so," he said. He sat up straighter and rolled his neck from one side to the other, a weak effort at easing the tension from sleeping in his desk chair. Glancing at his computer, he saw it was still on. Multiple screens were loaded with the searches he'd been working on last night.

Phoebe smiled softly and handed him a cup of coffee in the distinctive bright blue takeout cups from Roxanne's Country Store. He gratefully took it, immediately taking a swallow, the rich flavor welcome.

"Thank you," he said. "To what do I owe this morning gift?"

Phoebe plopped down in the chair on the opposite side of his desk. "I thought I'd check in since your car is covered in about a foot of snow. I figured you'd stayed late and fallen asleep." She paused, her dark brown eyes concerned. "You've been working so hard on this investigation since Callen died. I know how important it is, but I'm worried about you. It wouldn't hurt to take a break every so often," she said softly.

Jake took another sip of coffee and looked across his desk at Phoebe. She was a good friend. One of the few friends he could trust in the aftermath of the bombshell that had dropped in Catamount, Maine, a community along the vein of Maine forest through which the Appalachian Trail traversed. Just over a month ago, a mountain lion had been killed on a highway in Connecticut. Turned out, the mountain lion in question was a shifter from Catamount – Callen, a shifter from an old family of shifters. Jake's family was as old and storied as Callen's. Both were founding families of Catamount, one of the oldest and most well-protected shifter strongholds in the East.

As if Callen's death weren't devastating enough, Jake had started sleuthing in Callen's email accounts at the request of Callen's brother-in-law, Dane who also happened to be Jake's closest friend. Jake's expertise was computers, specifically writing code and hacking. Most of his hacking was above-board, but when needed, he could chase down almost anything. In this case, he wasn't so sure if that was a good thing or not. Though he still didn't know why Callen died on that highway, he knew Callen had been coordinating for Catamount shifters to be used for drug smuggling activities by someone out West. That nugget of knowledge had exploded into public view after Dane's new fiancée, Chloe, had been kidnapped to use as leverage last week. Chloe was safe and sound now, but no one knew who to trust because it was clear Callen hadn't been working alone.

While the shifter community had been reeling from Callen's death, they now had to grapple with an overwhelming sense of betrayal and fear. In the secretive world of shifters, trust was hard enough to come by. With shifter safety and existence at stake, Jake had been working relentlessly the last few weeks. Centuries of protection were at risk due to Callen's betrayal. Jake looked at Phoebe, taking in her dark eyes and long dark curls. Concern shone in her expression. He sighed. "I know, I know. I should take a break, but we have to get to the bottom of this. After what happened to Chloe..."

"Stop it," Phoebe ordered, cutting him off. "We all know Catamount shifters are in danger right now, but a few hours of sleep isn't going to change that. Plus, you're not much good to anyone if you can hardly keep your eyes open."

Jake grinned. "True. Well since I missed a good night's sleep last night, will you take my word for it that I promise I'll leave the office tonight by seven and go home?"

Phoebe shook her head. "Nope. I'll meet you here and make sure you leave. You're having dinner at my place tonight. After you have a decent meal, then I'll make sure you go home."

He chuckled. "You don't even trust me to go home afterwards?"

Phoebe smiled broadly. "Definitely not. I know you. You'll talk yourself into driving back to the office because you'll feel better after a decent meal. You need sleep, and I've decided to make sure you're going to get it. That's what friends are for," she said firmly.

Relief and appreciation washed through him. He'd

been pushing himself so hard, he couldn't remember the last time he'd had a decent meal. He'd even skipped Thanksgiving dinner yesterday because he'd been deep in the files of one of Callen's contacts out in Montana.

"Is Shana still staying with you?" he asked.

Shana was Dane's younger sister, Callen's widow, and Phoebe's best friend. She was completely devastated to learn about what Callen had been planning. Shana was a shifter as well, also from a founding family in Catamount. She was struggling to adjust to the knowledge that the man she loved had put the entire shifter community in Catamount at risk by revealing who, what, and where they were. Even worse, he'd planned to make money off of them. Shana had been staying with Phoebe since they discovered what happened to Callen.

Phoebe shook her head. "She said she felt like she had to face what happened. She moved into the old guesthouse on Dane's property. She's been over almost every day, but she's not staying with me anymore."

Jake nodded. After another swallow of coffee, he stood and stretched. "How about I take you to breakfast?"

"Only if you promise to meet me for dinner tonight and go home afterwards."

Jake couldn't help but smile. Phoebe was nothing if not protective of her friends. "I promise," he said firmly.

***

Phoebe absently ran her finger around the rim of her wineglass. "Well do you think the Fish & Wildlife guy in Montana is bad news or not?"

Jake arched a brow. "The problem is my gut tells me he's a good guy, but the computer trail isn't pretty. He was a main point of contact for Callen out there."

"So why do you think he's a good guy?"

Protected Mate (Catamount Lion Shifters)

Jake shrugged. "No good reason." He couldn't put his finger on it, but the man in question seemed to have discouraged Callen from something he was planning. The details were vague, but Jake just didn't get the sense the guy was in cahoots with Callen.

Phoebe pursed her lips. "Well, you can't trust him then."

Jake chuckled. "The list of people I trust is very short right now. I won't be adding anyone without extensive checking first. Aside from you, my parents, my sister, Dane, Shana, and Roxanne are about the only people on it."

Phoebe sighed and brushed her hair out of her face. True to his word, Jake had met her at his office and come to her place for dinner. He hadn't put up an argument when she insisted he ride with her. She looked across the table at him, and her heart clenched with worry. Jake was one of her best friends. She'd had a terrible crush on him in high school, what with his golden brown hair, bright blue eyes, sculpted face, and a hard body to die for. Phoebe hadn't dared let herself think he could ever be anything other than a friend. She wasn't a shifter, and Jake came from one of the oldest shifter families in town. Phoebe had cousins who were shifters, which is how her parents ended up Catamount, but she wasn't. So she'd taken her high school crush and tucked it away in a corner while Jake had become one of her closest friends.

In the shadowed light from the candles and the light over the stove, the feline cast to his features was more pronounced. His deep blue eyes tilted at the corners, his sensual mouth quirked when she stood to pick up their plates.

"I can get those," he said, starting to get up.

She put a hand on his shoulder. "Sit."

He chuckled. "It won't kill me to carry my plate to the dishwasher."

Phoebe opened the dishwasher and quickly put the dishes inside. When she turned back around, she found Jake right behind her. "Oh! I didn't hear you." She tried to check her pulse, but it raced ahead. He was too close for comfort.

His mouth quirked as he held up her wineglass. She took it from him. "I wasn't done yet."

He didn't reply and leaned against the counter. He was physically commanding in the small kitchen. He eyed her. "I kept my promise."

She wasn't sure what was happening with her, but Jake like this was crossing her signals and making her body run wild. After years and years of training herself to remember he could never be anything but a friend and keeping her body under strict control around him, it was as if she'd forgotten the hopelessness of letting herself want him. And oh, did she ever want him. Right now, in the dim, shadowy kitchen, heat coiled inside her belly and suffused her body. The claws of desire pricked her skin. Her heart beat wildly, her face flushed.

She looked up at Jake, praying her expression was composed. "You did. But you're not done yet."

His blue eyes held hers. If she hadn't known better, she'd have thought she saw desire darken them. But that was impossible, so she didn't even entertain the thought.

"I'm not?"

She shook her head, desperately trying to keep her wits while her pulse pounded and her body felt as if it were being pulled to him by a magnetic force. "You have to go home and sleep. No working tonight. That was the promise." She was breathless and barely managed to keep her voice level.

Protected Mate (Catamount Lion Shifters)

*You have got to stop this. Jake is off limits. You've
had it under control. Don't lose it now.*

Phoebe felt frantic inside. She needed to get her
wits about her. Jake pushed away from the counter and took
one stride, which brought him just in front of her. The heat
of his body tugged at hers. She tried to calm her heart rate,
but her body ignored her mind. *You're freaking out because
of this awful mess. You're just scared. That's what it is.
After what happened to Chloe, you're scared for everyone
in town, especially shifters. Jake could have been hurt
when he helped Dane rescue Chloe. That's all this is. Your
emotions are running wild.*

Upon the heels of this reasoning, Phoebe made the
stupid assumption that the heat would stop swirling inside
of her, her pulse would slow down, and she'd be able to
look at Jake without melting. When she looked up into his
dark blue eyes, molten heat built inside. The desire she'd
somehow kept in check for years ran rampant through her
body. Her heart pounded so hard, she feared he'd hear it.

She bit her lip and closed her eyes. They flew open
when she heard Jake swear softly. The moment her eyes
opened, his lips landed on hers. She was lost. He kissed her
fiercely, sweeping his tongue inside her mouth when she
gasped. She might as well have gone up in flames right
then and there. Years and years of denial lent a depth of
power to Jake's touch. His kiss nearly brought her to her
knees. One of his strong arms swept around her, sliding
down her back in a heated caress and cupping her bottom to
tug her against him. The hard, heated evidence of his
arousal pressed into the cradle of her hips.

Wet heat built inside of her, drenching her with
desire. Jake simply kept kissing her—hot, deep, openmouthed kisses. Their tongues tangled. She gasped for air
when he tore his lips from hers, his lips blazing a path

down her neck. Her name fell from his lips in a soft chant between nips and kisses. He swiftly unbuttoned her blouse, pausing for a long moment when he came to the black lace of her bra. Her nipples strained against the lace, tight and achy with want.

She could barely breathe, but she had to make this stop. It couldn't go further, or she wouldn't be able to face it when Jake realized this was a mistake, an aberration.

"Jake," she whispered furiously. "We have to stop."

His eyes were pinned to her breasts. Phoebe tried to step back, but the counter was behind her. She reached between them and tugged her blouse together, ignoring the desperate call of her body.

"Jake." She repeated his name, flinching at the hint of sadness in her voice.

He lifted his eyes to meet hers.

***

Jake stared at Phoebe, scrambling to gain purchase in his mind. She felt so good, so damn good. He'd wanted her for so long and was weary of denying himself. Yet, he couldn't have guessed at how phenomenal it would feel to touch her, to kiss her, to feel her flex under his touch, come alive in his arms. The cat in him stirred, the depth of his primal desire a living, breathing force he could barely keep leashed.

Phoebe said his name again, her voice tinged with the barest hint of sadness. He wanted to pull her close and tell her not to worry, there was nothing to be sad about. *This* force between them was about the only right and true thing in his life. But he'd denied his desire for her for so many years for good reason. When they were younger, he hadn't wanted to take advantage. That was only one reason for steering clear of her. He'd been raised a shifter among humans. Shifters had survived as they had by blending in. His family told tales of generations of shifters scrambling to survive until their numbers were enough that they could breathe easier. Though it had never been explicitly stated, Jake had grown up assuming he'd fall in love with another shifter. Then he'd stupidly fallen in lust with Naomi in college and realized what an utter disaster it could be for shifters to fall in love with humans. One stupid college relationship had led to far too many disastrous rumors. He'd sworn off even considering a relationship with any woman who wasn't a shifter. *But Phoebe's different. You know she's different.*

He could hardly bring himself to stop staring at her. He'd fantasized about her for years. Her generous breasts strained against the black lace of her bra, her nipples taut. Hints of pink peeked at him through the lace. He flicked his eyes to hers and saw the answering desire in hers. He knew, he'd known for years, that she wanted him as much as he wanted her. They'd done this dance of friends for so long, they were pretty good at it. But now, now that he'd had a taste of her, he couldn't stop. Not just yet.

Holding her gaze, he slipped his thumb under the clasp between her breasts. With a snap, the lace fell open, her breasts exposed to him. She gasped, her dark eyes wide. His eyes fell, his pulse pounding in his ears. Her breasts were round and full, the nipples dusky pink. Instinct drove him. He brought his hands up to curl around them, rubbing his thumbs over her peaked nipples. Her breath came in ragged gasps. He finally gave in and leaned forward to tug a nipple into his mouth, her sharp cry bringing his cat to quietly growl under the surface of his skin.

By the time he pulled away, both nipples were damp, glistening in the soft light in the kitchen. He was pulled tight with the depth of his want for her. He brought his eyes to hers again.

"Jake," she whispered. "We have to stop."

For once, he didn't want to listen to the bitter side of himself, the side that had told him for years he could never consider loving a woman who wasn't a shifter. Because they couldn't understand, they might betray him and his kind. With Phoebe, he knew that wasn't true. He trusted her completely.

He shook his head slowly. "But we don't. I know you want this as much as I do," he said softly.

Phoebe stood in front of him, her breasts rising and falling with her ragged breath. He dark hair tumbled in loose curls around her shoulders. Confusion and sadness flashed through her eyes. "I don't understand what's happening," she said.

"We're finally doing what we've both wanted to do for years." He stroked his hands down her shoulders and along her arms, his hands coming to rest at the juncture of her elbows. He wanted her with a depth beyond reason, but he knew if he didn't allow it to happen when she felt ready, it could devastate their friendship and ruin any chance for him to have what he'd denied himself for so long. A tiny, bitter corner of his mind pointed out that he was breaking his own rules here and he'd likely live to regret it.

"You've wanted to do this for years?" Phoebe asked.

Jake's heart clenched. He hid his feelings so well she didn't even know. He nodded slowly. "Yes."

She stared at him, her eyes skating over his face. She lifted her hand and carefully smoothed his brow, her finger trailing slowly down his cheek before it fell away. Her touch was a path of fire.

"Oh," she said.

She shimmied out from between his body and the

counter behind her. She pulled her blouse up around her shoulders, gripping the edges in front of her breasts. He had to bite his lip to keep from begging her not to hide herself from him. He watched her carefully, lust surging through him in waves. But with Phoebe, it wasn't merely lust. He loved her, had loved her for years, and he'd forced himself to ignore it, to keep her firmly in the category of friend. The list of reasons—she'd been too young at first, then she wasn't a shifter and all of his baggage about that—felt inconsequential now. The only thing that mattered was the humming pulse of electricity arcing between them.

Her eyes held confusion and concern. "Jake, this is…a lot. You're one of my best friends, and you've said for years that you'd never be with a woman who wasn't a shifter. I'm not a shifter. I can't risk our friendship over a night when you're tired and not thinking straight. Because the thing is, if we go further, I don't know if we can go back."

He closed his eyes and took a deep breath, reining his body in. He didn't want to stop, but he knew she had a point. He was beyond tired and felt rattled inside from recent events. He opened his eyes and met hers. He took another step, pausing in front of her again. He brushed a loose curl out of her eyes, tucking it behind her ear.

"Okay. We'll do this your way for tonight. I might be tired, but it doesn't change the fact that I've wanted you for too long."

Phoebe held his gaze, uncertainty flashing in hers. She nodded slowly. "You'll probably come to your senses after you get some sleep," she said wryly.

Jake traced her lips with his finger, savoring the hitch in her breath. "I finally came to my senses now. Take my word for it. This is only the beginning."

J.H. Croix

***

Phoebe walked to her car, snow crunching under her feet with each step. Snow had fallen again last night. The Maine woods were lovely, almost otherworldly, in the winter. The boughs of balsam and cedar trees were heavy with snow. The bare branches of oaks, elms and other hardwoods stood stark against the sky. A few stubborn leaves clung to the trees, their color faded, though bright against the white backdrop. She paused by her car and looked around. Snow created a soft, muted sense to the forest. A crow called, another answering quickly, their voices clear in the quiet. The sun was cresting in the sky, the snow sparkling where its light touched.

Driving in to work, her mind traveled back to last night with Jake. She'd driven him home, the car charged with electricity arcing between them. She was still stunned at what happened. After years of shoving her feelings for him into a tiny corner of her heart, never to be examined, never to be acted upon, he'd shattered the door to that hidden corner. His kiss, the feel of his hands on her body, and his words had been thrilling and terrifying at once. She couldn't quite believe he'd wanted her for years though he insisted he had. Part of her was frantic to take what he offered. Another part of her was frightened she'd lose one of her best friends if she acted on her desires. Years of hearing Jake's confident proclamations that he couldn't consider being with a woman who wasn't a shifter rang in her mind.

But, oh, how she wanted him. To hear him say he was tired of denying himself was music to her heart. She

128

pulled up at the hospital and hurried inside. She'd overslept after tossing and turning for most of the night. The interlude with Jake had electrified her, her mind and heart spinning in wild circles until she finally fell into an exhausted sleep.

"Hey Rosie," Phoebe called out as she walked past the nursing station and pushed through the swinging door into the break room.

"Hey girl!" Rosie's voice swung behind her into the room.

Phoebe quickly tugged her jacket off and stashed it in her locker. She switched out her winter boots for practical clogs. She was braiding her hair when Rosie entered the room a few minutes later. Rosie walked to the small round table in the center of the room and sat down with a sigh.

"It's not even nine yet, and I'm exhausted. Brought you a coffee," Rosie said.

Phoebe snapped an elastic band around the end of her braid and joined Rosie at the table.

"Ooh, you didn't just get me coffee, you stopped by Roxanne's and got my favorite. Thank you!" Phoebe took a swallow of the rich coffee from Roxanne's, closing her eyes and savoring the flavor. When she opened them, she looked across at Rosie. Rosie was a good friend. They'd met in nursing school. Rosie had grown up in a nearby town and moved to Catamount when she got a job at the local hospital. She was like Phoebe, in that she was distantly related to some shifters, but wasn't one herself. Rosie had short, curly golden hair with bright blue eyes. She looked sweet and innocent, but her mischievous smile gave away her sly sense of humor.

Rosie ran a hand through her curls and eyed Phoebe. "Any word from Shana?"

Phoebe shook her head. Phoebe loved the fact that she got to work with two of her closest friends, Rosie and Shana. But lately, she and Rosie mostly worried about Shana, unsure how to help other than to simply be there however they could. Shana had yet to return to work since her husband, a shifter, died on a highway in Connecticut for reasons that remained mysterious. After staying with Phoebe for a few weeks, Shana had insisted she needed to try to be on her own again and moved into a small guesthouse on her brother's property.

"She's on the schedule for tomorrow," Rosie said. "I'm hoping it'll be good for her to have something to focus on other than Callen's death and everything else that's been going on."

"I think it'll help her. She needs to get out of her head for a bit. I wish this mess would blow over, but it's not looking like it will anytime soon."

Rosie shook her head slowly. "Far as I can tell, the mess has only begun."

"How much worse could it get?"

Rosie threw a hard glance her way. "Um, let's see. Callen died on a highway in mountain lion form. No one knows why the hell he didn't shift back. Then Jake stumbles onto the bombshell that Callen was working with God-only-knows-who to sell the services of Catamount shifters to smuggle drugs. As if that wasn't bad enough, Chloe gets kidnapped by some shifter from out of town and Callen's little brother. Let's not forget that Chloe just happens to be the woman Dane fell head over heels in love with. Dane who's from one of the oldest known shifter families in Catamount and Shana's brother. He's so close to the middle of this, I don't know how he stands the heat. Thank God, Dane and Jake handled Chloe's kidnapping as fast as they did! So, if you're wondering how much worse it could get, I'm thinking we've got a long way to go before this is over."

Phoebe groaned. "I know, I know, I know. I was trying to convince myself it couldn't get any worse. But it's bad. I wish there was something I could do to help."

Rosie sipped her coffee. "Be the good friend you are and just be there. Shana needs you and Jake needs you."

The intercom beeped. "Give me the quick update from rounds this morning," Phoebe said, referring to the early-morning medical rounds that occurred prior to her shift starting.

After a summary of nothing out of the ordinary, Rosie dropped a little bombshell. "Oh, and the new guy here—we think he's a shifter trying to hide it."

Anxiety coiled inside. "What are you talking about?" Phoebe asked in a hiss.

Rosie glanced around quickly. "New patient. He says he's here on vacation and having chest pains. But he feels like a shifter to me. He's in the room at the end of the hall. Check on him and let me know what you think."

Though Phoebe wanted to run down the hall and immediately scope out the man Rosie mentioned, she forced herself to act normal. After doing her usual check-ins with patients from the day before, she made her way down the hall. She found the man in question sitting up in bed watching a cooking show on television. At a glance, she'd have guessed him to be a shifter. Though she wasn't one herself, she'd lived her entire life in Catamount surrounded by them. There were the obvious signs, such as the cat-like eyes and a feline cast to his face. Along with the less obvious signs, such as a distinct feline quality to the way the man lounged in bed and the subtle primal quality to the way he looked at her. In a flash, she recalled Jake's bright blue eyes last night when he'd pulled back from their kiss—dark with passion, a focus so intense it sent shivers up her spine just thinking about it.

"Excuse me?" the man asked.

Phoebe realized she'd zoned out and turned her attention back to the man. He had dark blonde hair and slate gray eyes. She made a point of checking his medical chart by the bed and checked his vitals. The name on the chart was Paul Malone though Phoebe's 'uh-oh' radar was so strong, she doubted that was his actual name. Nonetheless...

"So Paul, how are you feeling today?" Phoebe asked as she entered his blood pressure rating in his chart.

"Okay, I guess. Yesterday was pretty scary."

Phoebe watched him as the man launched into a vague summary of his physical state, increasing her doubt that he had anything wrong with him. But she listened and observed, wondering if Rosie's suspicions were correct, and if so, what would he want by checking himself into the hospital. Phoebe's primary concern was that he was after information on any one of the many shifters who worked in the hospital. Shana was a nurse while her brother Dane was one of the back-up emergency room doctors. They were only two of many shifters who were in and out of the hospital throughout the week.

"So, you said you were visiting Catamount. How long do you plan to be here?" Phoebe asked after Paul finished talking.

Paul's gray eyes bounced to the window and back to her before he replied. "Not sure. I heard it was a nice place. Thought I'd check it out."

Though Catamount saw its share of visitors in the spring, summer and fall due to its proximity to the Appalachian Trail and its extensive orchards, visitors in winter were much less likely. There was a ski lodge in a nearby town, which tended to draw most of the winter visitors. Phoebe couldn't help herself. "This time of year doesn't bring too many tourists here. Do you have family nearby?"

Paul's eyes tightened, but he kept his expression bland. "I like winter. No reason not to visit just because of that." He turned his focus back to the television, the message loud and clear that Phoebe was dismissed.

Later that afternoon, she walked outside with Rosie after their shift was over. "Well, I'm with you on that guy. I'd bet money he's a shifter. Why is he here and why this hospital? I'm stopping by Jake's office now, and I'll make sure this gets passed on to Hank and Dane."

Rosie climbed into her car with a wave. "Call me if you hear anything. See you tomorrow."

Phoebe headed directly to Jake's office. As soon as she walked in, desire slammed into her body, disorienting her. All of her promises to herself that she'd be able to put their kiss behind her went up in smoke. Jake was looking at his computer screen and ran a hand through his hair. He didn't appear to have heard her come in. For a moment, she allowed herself to enjoy the sight of him. Even hunched over a desk, his body was pure masculinity. He wore a soft t-shirt that stretched across his back, the corded muscles along his spine standing out, his strong shoulders taut under the fabric. She wanted to walk over and drop a kiss on the soft spot where the curve of his neck met the bulk of his shoulder.

He suddenly straightened and swiveled in his chair, his eyes snapping to hers instantly, his intense blue gaze igniting sparks inside of her. Less than five seconds had passed, and her breath was short, molten heat swirled in her center, and she lost focus. It didn't help that Jake's eyes darkened the moment he saw her, desire flashing in them.

His primal gaze set butterflies amassing in her belly.

"Hey," he said gruffly.

"Hey." Her one word greeting hung in the air, as she stood frozen inside his office.

All the reasons why she'd kept her feelings for Jake tucked tightly in a corner raced through her thoughts. She forced her eyes away from his, tracking the movement of a cardinal outside flitting in the trees. Its bright red plumage glowed amidst the snowy skeleton of the trees. This is what she'd wanted to avoid—the discomfort, and the worry that he saw the depth of her feelings for him beyond the heat of the moment. Above all, he was one of her best friends. If she lost his friendship, she would be devastated. She was startled out of her train of thought by his voice.

"Phoebe."

The cardinal flew from one branch to another, and she brought her eyes back to Jake. Her belly did a somersault. She couldn't seem to force her body to obey her. Years and years of habit should have kicked in, but the kisses they shared last night had blown her control to bits.

"Whatever you're thinking, stop it," Jake said flatly.

His stark words had the intended effect of knocking her mind off its loop. "How about you stop trying to read my mind?" she countered, irritated at how easily he could read her.

He stood from his chair and moved fluidly around his desk coming to a stop in front of her. He leaned his hips against the desk and reached for her hands, which were cold from the snow-chilled air. The feel of his warm, strong hands around hers caused her breath to draw sharply. Her pulse went wild again, but she couldn't have looked away from his gaze if she wanted.

His hair was rumpled as if he'd run his hands through it repeatedly. His eyes were still tired, though not as weary as they'd been yesterday. Her heart tumbled. The worry she held for him had been constant ever since news had come about Callen's death. None of them could have realized that event was only a harbinger of more to come.

Jake rubbed his thumb across the back of her palm. "I wasn't trying to read your mind. How about we agree not to freak out about last night?"

Relief washed through her. Jake understood. He was trying to get them back on friends-only footing, which was exactly where they needed to be. On the heels of relief came a sharp pain, the pain she'd been trying to avoid for years. A less than five-minute span last night, and the heartbreak she'd tried to avoid for years was in front of her. Because dammit, he'd give her a reason to hope. And no matter how many times she told her heart it wasn't a good idea to hope, her heart ignored her.

Phoebe nodded. "Right. I'm all about not freaking out about last night. It was an aberration. We're friends, we've been friends for years and that won't change."

He shook his head slowly. "That's not what I meant about not freaking out."

Her belly flip-flopped. "What…what did you mean?"

"I meant let's not freak out about what happened because it's absolutely okay. We kissed because we wanted to. I plan to kiss you again…"

Her breath whooshed out of her lungs, and her pulse ricocheted wildly. For a second, her heart flew with joy and longing streaked through her. On the heels of that, she tried to talk her feelings down. She couldn't let herself think this could be real. It hurt enough to pretend her feelings didn't exist, it would be far, far worse to water them with false hopes. "Jake, we can't…"

His thumb stilled its soft strokes. His eyes

narrowed, pinned to hers. "Who says we can't?"

When she opened her mouth to reply, Jake released one of her hands and put his finger to her lips. "Tell me you didn't want that kiss," he said, his voice gruff.

Phoebe tried to form the words to tell him she hadn't wanted that kiss, but she couldn't because it was an out and out lie. She closed her eyes and took a deep breath. When she opened them again, Jake's finger traced the contours of her mouth before his hand fell away. Her lips tingled at his soft touch.

"Okay. So now that we got that out of the way, what brings you here?" he asked with a small smile.

She couldn't help the smile that bloomed in her heart, her lips following suit. Just when she thought he was going to push too far, he backed off easily and gave her the emotional space she needed.

"Oh yeah, I came by to tell you we think we have a shifter who checked himself into the hospital."

Jake arched a brow. "And that would be a problem, why? Half the people in town are mountain lion shifters."

"He's from out of town and damn vague. Says he came for a visit and had chest pains yesterday. Rosie saw him first before I got to work and then I checked on him. He's laying low, but I have a bad feeling. I can't think of anything other than bad reasons for him to want to be in the hospital. Shana and Dane both work there, not to mention that plenty of other staff are shifters. We need to talk to Hank and Dane."

Jake swore and dropped her hands. He leaned backwards on his desk and snatched his phone up, making two calls in quick succession. He left messages for Hank and Dane to call right away and set his phone down. He turned back to her.

"Okay, here's the deal, none of you are to be alone

with him. We don't know who he's working with, or who he's after. Once I talk to Hank, I'll see if he can set up a security rotation. How long will he be at the hospital?"

"That's the thing, there's no good reason to keep him, but he keeps reporting vague symptoms that we have to run tests on. I think it's better if he's there because we can keep an eye on him."

Jake nodded. "Definitely. Dammit! I was hoping whoever was connected to Seth and Randall would want to stay away after what happened with Chloe. I mean, Seth and Randall are in jail and won't be going anywhere else soon." He pushed away from the desk and began pacing. "You're going to have to keep a close eye on who goes in and out of that room. That might help us sift through who's working with them here in Catamount." He paused and looked at her for a long moment. "Promise me you won't go in his room alone again. For all we know, they're targeting anyone close to those they're after. You're close to Dane, Shana and almost everyone important in the shifter families here. Promise me."

Phoebe nodded. "I promise. Rosie and I already talked about it after I saw him today." Cold fear chased up her spine, and she shivered, hugging her arms around her waist. She caught Jake's eyes. "I wish we knew more."

He stopped pacing in front of her and leaned against the desk, tugging her into him. Before she could think, he'd wrapped her in his strong, sure embrace. The heat of his body seeped into hers. She leaned her forehead against his shoulder with a sigh. Between the ever-present state of vigilance she'd been in ever since Chloe had been kidnapped and weeks of worry about everything, she was relieved to soak in his reassuring warmth and comfort.

***

137

Jake studied the grain of wood in the floor inside the police station. The building was centuries old and retained the original hardwood oak flooring, worn from years of feet traveling across it, yet still rich in color. Dane was on the phone with Chloe while they waited for Hank. Dane finished his call and slipped his phone in his pocket. He glanced to Jake.

"Every time I think about the mess Callen created, I wish he was still alive so I could make him pay," Dane said, shaking his head, his eyes weary and angry at once.

Jake leaned his head against the wall behind his chair and sighed. "You and me both. How's Chloe?"

"She's good. She's getting annoyed with me checking in all the time, but she's putting up with it so far." Dane paused, his eyes darkening. "I'm relieved she's okay, but I'm not going to breathe easy until we get to the bottom of this."

The door to Hank's office opened and he waved them inside. "Come on in, guys."

Jake and Dane sat in two chairs across from Hank's desk. Hank took a swig of coffee and turned his gaze to Jake. "So what's up at the hospital?"

Jake quickly filled them in, along with the latest update from his online forays. "I'm thinking one of us needs to head to Montana. As it stands, we're on the defensive on this side while they keep showing up here. Let's get out in front. I've found enough clues online to point us to the right locations. Hell, I can pinpoint the locations of every ISP address linked to the accounts Callen was emailing. Maybe they're fronts, but everything leads somewhere."

Hank glanced between Jake and Dane and shrugged. "I'm with you there, but I can't go. It's gonna have to be someone else. Hate to say it, but we can't send either one of you. You're too prominent. Plus, if they didn't know your faces before, they do now. Both of you were all over the news after Chloe's kidnapping."

Dane swore and looked to Jake. "Any ideas?"

Jake shook his head. "Not yet. Let me think on it."

They moved on to developing a plan for surveillance at the hospital. It twisted Jake's gut that every time they considered the threats shifters were facing, they came face to face with the reality that Callen had recruited within the Catamount Clan. His youngest brother, Randall who'd always been eager to impress Callen, was an easy mark, but they couldn't assume others weren't involved. Sussing out whom they could trust was a complicated task.

Jake walked outside later to find snow drifting down. The police station was in the center of town on one of the streets adjacent to the town green. He crossed the street and walked onto the path that led to the center of the green, leaving footsteps in the fresh layer of snow. It was late afternoon with the sun low in the sky. The bare tree branches cast a network of shadows on the snow. The plump snowflakes glittered as they drifted through the lingering rays of sun angling across the green. He thought of Phoebe, his heart feeling a primal tug. He turned on his heel and walked quickly back to his truck. He needed to see her. *Now.*

As he drove toward her house, a corner of his mind tried to remind him why he'd told himself he'd only be with a shifter. His college girlfriend, Naomi, had been the one and only woman he'd been involved with who wasn't a shifter. He'd fallen so hard and fast for her, he'd ignored the warning signs. She'd been overly dramatic and often portrayed herself as a victim of any number of circumstances. Jake's hormones found her so phenomenal, he'd charged ahead, thinking she needed someone like him and enjoying the superficial pleasure derived from feeling like her hero. In a haze of hormonal overdrive, convinced they were meant to be together, he'd told her who and what he was. She'd promptly gone into drama central mode and flipped out. He'd spent months clearing up rumors and feeling like a complete idiot. The saving grace had been she'd transferred to another college in the aftermath. To this day, he didn't know if she'd done so because she was legitimately afraid of him because he was a shifter, or because she hadn't counted on how many friends he and the other shifters had who were willing to close ranks around them.

He'd stayed true to his commitment to only get involved with shifters since then, but he'd yet to find anyone who called to him. Except Phoebe. She'd always had a straight line to his heart. When he was younger and watched her grow into the beautiful woman she'd become, he'd told himself he couldn't take advantage of her. She was four years behind him in school. The yawning gap between their ages then was nothing now with him at thirty-four and Phoebe at thirty. Between the time he tried to keep from fawning all over Phoebe and his messy brush with Naomi, he never managed to wipe out the shimmering electric connection that hummed to life every time he was near Phoebe.

He might not be thinking too clearly right now, but he was damn tired of denying himself what he wanted. Especially when, in the midst of the suspicions running high in Catamount, Phoebe was one of the few who held his absolute faith. He turned into the driveway to her house in the wispy light of dusk. Her house was a cape style

home, painted a soft cream with the whimsical touch of
purple trim and a matching purple steel roof. Snow was
falling more heavily now, coating the landscape. Phoebe's
car wasn't in the drive yet, so Jake texted her quickly
asking when she'd be home. Moments later, she replied to
report she was on her way. He leaned his head back and
watched the snow float down over the field beside her
house. A small creek meandered through the field, the dark
ribbon of it glimmering under the last rays of sun.

    Phoebe's holiday lights came on. Jake chuckled to
himself, realizing she must have them set on a timer. Her
home was laced with holiday lights along the roof with two
bare trees flanking her front walk decorated as well. Phoebe
pulled up and waved at him from her car. He climbed out
and followed her down the snow-covered slate path to her
front entrance. When she reached the door, she turned to
him. Her dark hair was flecked with snowflakes. One
caught on her lashes, glittering bright under the lights by
the door.

    "I didn't know you were stopping by," she said, a
question in her eyes.

    She blinked and the snowflake on her lashes
disappeared. Her dark eyes met his, and his breath hitched.

    "I hope you're not planning to ask me to leave."

    She shook her head and tugged her keys out of her
purse. "Of course not. Come on in."

    She nudged the door with her shoulder once she
unlocked it. Jake's eyes fell to the flimsy lock on her door.
He needed to beef up the locks on her house. In Catamount,
it had never crossed his mind to worry about the state of
anyone's locks. He hated that he had to think this way, but
right now all he wanted was to make sure those close to
him were safe. They'd gotten lucky with how quickly
they'd been able to handle Chloe's kidnapping. He didn't

want to be caught blindsided again.

He shut the door behind him and locked it. Phoebe dropped her purse and bag on the couch as she walked into the kitchen, flicking on lamps along the way. The air was cool. He glanced at the woodstove in the corner of her living room.

"I'm going to start a fire, okay?" he called out.

She leaned her head around the archway leading into the kitchen. "Please do," she said with a grin.

Jake eyed the small wood rack nearby and turned to head outside. In the snowy almost-dark, he headed for the woodshed on the side of her yard. Walking through the light cast from her festive holiday lights, he methodically stacked wood on the holder outside her front door, filling it to capacity before bringing an armful inside. Once he had the fire started in the woodstove, Phoebe called to him from the kitchen. He walked in to find her ladling stew into bowls, instantly handing him one when he stepped to her side.

"I made it in the slow-cooker this morning. I didn't know the weather would be ideal for beef stew," she said.

She nudged him to the table and followed him over with a bowl. Jake uncorked the bottle of red wine on the table and filled the wineglasses she'd set out.

"This is amazing," he said a few minutes later between bites of the rich, savory stew.

Phoebe grinned. "I didn't know you'd be enjoying it with me, so I'm glad you like it."

"Not that there'd be any doubt. You're a damn good cook," he replied. He'd shared many meals with Phoebe and knew her to be ridiculously good at cooking and baking. She didn't go for fancy, but could make the simplest meals amazing. He finished his bowl and pushed it away. Leaning back in his chair, he looked over at her. Her dark curls were damp from the snow, her cheeks flushed. Her dark eyes drew him into their depths. All the years he'd known her, he'd vigilantly shut his brain off when it came to thinking about what it would feel like to experience the passion she exuded. She approached most everything with zeal—cooking, hiking, sewing, nursing, and more. With her dark hair and eyes, curvy figure and warm smile, he'd spent years longing to know her beyond the friendship they shared.

Watching her now, he let go of the tight control he'd kept on his feelings for her. He simply didn't care to hide them anymore. He sensed she didn't quite believe him, but he didn't know what to do about that other than show her. When she stood to carry dishes to the sink, he followed her with the empty wineglasses. The clink of dishes and silverware placed in the sink echoed in the quiet room.

Jake's body was humming. After so many years of tamping down the ever-present arc of desire for Phoebe, to allow it to exist freely set him afire. After handing her the wineglasses and feeling the brush of her fingers against the back of his palm in the tiny exchange, he had to close his eyes to keep from yanking her against him. When she finally turned to him, he reached for her hands. Her dark eyes widened, but she didn't say anything. He began walking backwards, drawing her with him into the living room. The light from the fire in the woodstove flickered through the glass door. Snow was still falling outside, the white flakes shining brightly in the glow from the holiday lights encircling the house.

He backed up until his legs bumped the back of the couch. Resting his hips on the edge, he tugged her close, barely able to keep himself under control. The act of letting go of his iron control on his feelings for her was unnerving. The cat in him purred and growled softly, desperate to unleash the lust surging through him. He lifted a hand and trailed the back of it down her cheek, into the soft dip of her neck, across her collarbone and over the lush curve of her breast. Her breath hitched. He flicked his eyes to her face to see her tongue dart out to moisten her lips. The thin thread of control loosened further.

Available now!

Chosen Mate (Catamount Lion Shifters, Book 2)

Be sure to sign up for my newsletter! I promise - no spam! If you sign up, you'll get notices on new releases at discounted prices   and information on upcoming books. Go here to sign up: http://jhcroix.com/page4/

Protected Mate (Catamount Lion Shifters)

Thank you for reading Protected Mate (Catamount Lion Shifters)! I hope you enjoyed the story. If so, you can help other readers find my books in a variety of ways.

1) Write a review!
2) Sign up for my newsletter, so you can receive information about upcoming new releases at http://jhcroix.com/page4/
3) Follow me on Twitter at https://twitter.com/JHCroix
4) Like my Facebook page at https://www.facebook.com/jhcroix
5) Like and follow my Amazon Author page at https://amazon.com/author/jhcroix

***
Catamount Lion Shifters

Protected Mate

Chosen Mate

Fated Mate

Destined Mate

Ghost Cat Shifters

The Lion Within

Lion Lost & Found

Diamond Creek Alaska Novels

When Love Comes

J.H. Croix

Follow Love

Love Unbroken

Love Untamed

Tumble Into Love

Last Frontier Lodge Novels

Christmas on the Last Frontier

Love at Last

Just This Once

Falling Fast

Acknowledgments

I'll keep it simple. My husband's support is endless. Laura Kingsley edits my work like a champ, holding me to a higher standard every time. CT Cover Creations works wonders and creates my amazing covers. And of course, my readers…you are so kind, supportive and fabulous!

J.H. Croix

Author Biography

Bestselling author J. H. Croix lives in a small town in the historical farmlands of Maine with her husband and two spoiled dogs. Croix writes sexy contemporary romance and steamy paranormal romance with strong independent women and rugged alpha men who aren't afraid to show some emotion. Her love for quirky small-towns and the characters that inhabit them shines through in her writing. Take a walk on the wild side of romance with her bestselling novels!